Exe On The Beach

Lockwood and Darrow 6

Suzy Bussell

Exe on the Beach

Lockwood and Darrow Book 6

By Suzy Bussell

This is a work of fiction. All of the characters, organisations, and events portrayed in this novel are either products of the author's imagination or are used fictitiously.

This book has been written and edited using British English.

Chapter One

Angus Darrow and Charlotte Lockwood, private detectives in Devon, strolled on the esplanade in Exmouth, on their way to their next case.

It was eleven thirty in the morning on a warmer than usual July day. The residents and tourists in Devon had enjoyed an early summer in June, and now the popular seaside resort of Exmouth, ten miles south of Exeter, was preparing itself for the usual onslaught of summer holiday visitors bound for the seafront and the sandy beach.

Exmouth had got its name because it was where the River Exe and the English Channel met. A big town, it attracted tourists even off-season.

"This is the first time we've been to Exmouth together," Charlotte commented. The soft breeze from the sea played with her blonde hair, lifting it off her shoulders. She was dressed in a black denim jacket, crisp white shirt, and dark jeans, with a slim Cartier watch on her left wrist.

Angus glanced at her. "I come here sometimes with the running club. They like to mix things up occasionally with a run on the beach." Always smart, he was dressed in a dark-grey three-piece suit and tie.

"Isn't that hard?"

"The sand here isn't as bad as the pebbles farther down the coast. There's a parkrun in Seaton and they start and end on the pebbles."

"Have you done it?" Charlotte grimaced at the thought of running, let alone on pebbles.

"Not yet, but it's on my list of things to do this year." Now in his early fifties, Angus was fit, and enjoyed the benefits of running: both getting out in nature and the dopamine afterwards.

"I used to love coming to Exmouth when I was a child." Charlotte stopped and looked out over the expanse of the sea. "We used to come here from Hertfordshire every year and visit my grandmother in her great big house in Topsham."

"Which is now your great big house?"

Charlotte's house was a few miles north. Topsham was a small town between Exmouth and Exeter, and her house, the largest and most envied, looked out over the Exe.

"It is. Mum and Dad couldn't afford holidays abroad or even in this country, so we'd stay with my gran every summer. She didn't mind, though. And she never treated us any differently from the posh side of the family."

Angus smiled. "The posh side?"

"Mum's family were all posh. Well, comparatively: upper middle class. When she married my dad, people thought he was a bit of rough because he was working class. She was happy, though. We all were."

Angus mused for a moment. "Maybe we crossed paths all those years ago, here on the beach."

They paused to take in the scenery. The sandy beach stretched before them, a full two miles. Lining the seafront were houses and hotels, interspersed with cafés and restaurants. The relaxed atmosphere lent itself to both family outings and casual strolls. It was a pleasant, unpretentious area, free from frills.

"Did you come to Exmouth often too?" Charlotte asked.

"Sometimes. In the summer, mainly. I'd get the train with my brother, Duncan, and some friends from Exeter and doss around on the beach."

Charlotte laughed. "I can't imagine you dossing around."

"Oh, I did. Nothing illegal, mind, just lazing about. Kicking a ball around on the beach, a bit of swimming. That sort of thing."

"Have you ever thought about moving here?"

Angus pondered her question. "I hadn't – but I might see if I can find my next property to develop around here. I'll look at prices. There's no shortage of potential tenants, just like Exeter."

"It seems to be taking you a long time to find another property to work on," Charlotte observed.

Angus had left the police a few years before, and to supplement his pension, he had converted an old pharmacy into rental flats. He had done a small amount of private detective work when it came up, but when he started working with Charlotte, things had really taken off. Her cybersecurity skills were among the best in the country, and she'd proved herself valuable beyond words.

"There's a good reason for that," he told her. "The properties are either too expensive to start with, or someone outbids me."

Charlotte clapped her hands together. "I do like a good auction."

Angus combined a smile and an eyeroll.

"What's that for?"

"Of course you love an auction – you're a multimillionaire."

Charlotte grinned. "That doesn't matter. I loved them before I was rich. But yes, it's much easier to outbid people these days."

They carried on walking until they arrived at their destination: Oceanique was a modern building overlooking the sea, only a few years old. It housed one of the country's most exclusive seafood restaurants, owned and run by celebrity chef Lawrence Westwood. It drew customers from far and wide: most of them hoping they would get a glimpse of the man they'd watched rustle up delicious meals on TV. He was a tour de force in the restaurant industry, who'd worked his way up from being a trainee chef to one of the most famous faces on TV.

"Do you think Lawrence will be here?" Charlotte asked, surveying the outside of the building. "I'd love to meet him."

"I'm not sure. It was his wife I spoke to. She wouldn't say what it was about on the phone, just that she'd like us to call round."

"Have you seen him on TV? I've seen a few of his shows. He's really popular because of his passion for combining simple recipes with top ingredients."

Angus thought for a moment. "I've seen some episodes. Didn't he run that campaign to help support farmers against the supermarkets?"

"He did. I saw that. And he got a lot of stick for it too. If you're a celebrity, you aren't allowed a political opinion."

"Your ex-husband gets away with it," Angus commented.

Charlotte frowned. "Thank you very much for reminding me. I'd managed nearly three days without thinking about Idris, which is a record for me, and now I'm back to day zero."

"Sorry. I thought you'd put all that behind you?"

She grimaced. "Most days, I have. But sometimes it's still a struggle. I don't see how you can get on so well with your ex-wife, Rhona." Charlotte waved a dismissive hand. "Yes, I do remember what you told me about your break-up, but it's ridiculous how you've managed to rise above it all. What's your secret?"

Angus looked Charlotte straight in the eye. "Our situation was completely different. Neither of us had had an affair, let alone with the other's best friend. So I don't have a strong reason to think badly of her."

Charlotte considered this. "I suppose if Idris and me had just drifted apart, then I'd feel differently. The betrayal was the hardest thing."

"I'll remember not to mention Idris again." He smiled. "I'll call him *he who should not be named* instead."

Charlotte laughed. "This is not Harry Potter!"

Angus looked up at the restaurant in front of them. "We'd better go in."

They approached the main entrance. A Closed sign dangled on the glass door. They both shielded their eyes with their hands and peered inside. Chairs upholstered in navy-blue velvet made a plush contrast to the crisp white tablecloths. Framed maritime art hung on the walls. An elegant bar area at one end of the restaurant was stocked with an array of high-end spirits.

A woman in her sixties was sitting at one of the tables, tapping at a laptop. "I guess that's her?" Charlotte said.

Angus knocked gently on the glass.

The woman looked up, then stood up smoothly and came towards them.

Chapter Two

Cressida Westwood unlocked the door of Oceanique and opened it, an inquisitive look on her face. She was a larger-than-average woman, at least five foot ten, with dark-blonde hair and brown eyes. She wore leggings with an oversized shirt that skimmed her thighs. "Mr Darrow?" Her gaze darted to Charlotte for a moment.

"Yes, and this is my colleague, Charlotte Lockwood."

"Come in." She opened the door wider and they stepped in. She locked the door behind them, then indicated the table she had been sitting at. A faint, not unpleasant smell of cooked seafood scented the air. The whole restaurant seemed a peaceful oasis.

"Do sit down, please. I was just doing a spot of accounts. It's never-ending." She rolled her eyes. "Can I get you a coffee or tea?" Her accent was home counties posh.

"We're good, thanks," Angus replied, answering for them both.

Cressida raised her eyebrows, then looked at Charlotte, who shook her head.

Angus took his notebook and pen from his inner jacket pocket and put them on the table. "How can we help?"

"Straight to it!" Cressida studied him as she mused. "Well, I suppose there's no beating about the bush. You'll have heard of my husband, of course. Lawrence Westwood. Celebrity chef, TV personality, local man who did good, etcetera etcetera."

Charlotte and Angus both nodded. Of course, she was right. Everyone over the age of thirty in the UK had heard of Lawrence Westwood.

"I take it that, as Lawrence isn't here, you don't want him to know you're talking to us," Angus said.

"Actually, I don't mind him knowing. Not at all. The reason why I've called you in is that he's gone missing." Her tone was matter of fact at such an important piece of information.

"Right. Okay." Angus paused for a moment to process the way in which Cressida had announced this news.

"And before you ask, I haven't told the police." Cressida waved a hand.

Angus frowned. "Why is that?"

"He's done this before, three or four times. He gets super-stressed, disappears for a few days to reset himself, then comes back all guns blazing and acting as though nothing has happened. But this time it's been over a week now, and people are starting to ask questions. People expect him to be here in the restaurant at least a few nights of the week. They love to come looking for him in the kitchen and take a selfie."

"Is there somewhere he usually goes when he does this?" Angus asked.

"Yes and no. The first time was a spa hotel in Cumbria,

the second, a glamping tent on a nice site in Wales. Actually, I think he went to the tent twice..."

"So you want us to find him?" Angus started mapping out a plan in his mind.

"Yes, I need him back. This place can run without him for a while, but not for ever."

"Has he had any support for his mental health issues before this?" Charlotte asked.

"Yes, of course. And it has helped, but he lets things get on top of him. It's like a slippery slope. He won't talk about his problems usually. Stiff upper lip and all that, then, slowly but surely, something tips the balance and he's back to where he was before." She rubbed her eyes. "It's just – this time, I hadn't noticed how quickly he'd declined."

Charlotte looked away and took a deep breath. Angus suspected she was struggling to keep her thoughts on the matter to herself. Then she glanced at him. "We'll need a list of friends and family he might have gone to. Did he take his mobile phone?"

"Yes, but it isn't switched on. I've tried ringing it."

"Do you have the app that lets you track his location?"

Cressida's eyes narrowed. "No. I wouldn't have that, on principle. It's as good as stalking."

"Has he called you at all?" Angus asked.

"No."

"And you're sure that he's left of his own accord and he's safe?"

"You mean, has something untoward happened?" She laughed. "No. I know Lawrence. He's got himself in a pickle and he wants time out, but I need him back here."

Angus made some notes, and Cressida watched. "I need you to keep this strictly confidential," she said. "If word gets out, the press will have a field day."

"You can rely on our complete discretion. What message did he leave when he left?"

"He didn't leave a message; he never does. Look, he's done it before," Cressida huffed. "I know he's all right. He's just hiding somewhere and in need of help, so I need you to find him toot sweet." Her tone was almost exasperated, as though she resented having to explain herself.

Angus twiddled his pen in his fingers, pondering. "Does he have a therapist or counsellor?"

Cressida gave a small laugh. "Ha! No, he doesn't. Lawrence doesn't like that sort of thing: dwelling on your feelings and making a mountain out of a molehill. The help he had in the past wasn't therapy like that. It was pulling himself together and getting on with things after we went on a holiday. We both think it's better to put the past behind you and get on with the future."

Not that that seems to be working, thought Angus. "We'll need his phone number, a list of friends' names and addresses, and anywhere that you think he might have gone, even if it's a slim chance. And we'll need his laptop and iPad too."

"He doesn't have either of those. He's a total techno-phobe. He hates computers: says they're the scourge of society."

Charlotte blinked. Angus knew exactly what she was thinking. "That's disappointing," Charlotte said, "as an elec-tronic trail is the easiest to follow." She nodded towards Cressida's phone. "I need to install an app on your phone which records calls. If Lawrence rings you, it will record the voice conversation and extract as much information as it can about where the call came from."

Cressida handed over her phone. Charlotte took her tablet computer from her bag and linked Cressida's phone to it. With a few clicks, the app was installed and the phone handed back.

"You can start straight away, can't you? That's what you said on the phone."

"We can," Angus replied. "We'll get straight to it. Before that, though, I need you to go through everything you can remember of the last twenty-four hours before Lawrence disappeared." Angus's pen was poised over his notepad.

Cressida took off her reading glasses and placed them on the table, then put her hand over them for a moment. "He worked here the night before. It was full to the rafters."

"Any issues?"

"No. It was an ordinary sitting and everyone was finished by eleven pm."

"Did you go home together?"

"Yes. After a few drinks here with our head chef, we left at about one. And no, we didn't drink and drive. He drank, I drove. I haven't touched alcohol since I hit the menopause. It gives me horrible hot flushes even now."

"Was everything normal when you got home?"

"Yes. In the morning, he answered some messages and made a few phone calls."

"Do you know who he rang?" Angus asked.

"No. And no, I didn't ask. I never ask."

"Where is your house?"

"It's a farmhouse on the outskirts of Exmouth, near the border with Budleigh Salterton. It only takes ten minutes to get there if the traffic is light."

"When did he leave home?"

"Just after lunch he said he was going to visit the boat. He left at one, and that was the last time I saw him."

"The boat?"

bought it a few years ago, and it supplies most of the seafood we serve in the restaurant. All seasonal, of course."

"Who's the captain?"

"The skipper's name is Remy Le Gall."

Angus made a note to visit Remy first.

"Did Lawrence say what time he'd be home?"

"No. He usually got back around four, then went to the restaurant at around five."

"That seems quite late."

Cressida shook her head. "Well, Scott Whelton does the day-to-day running of the restaurant. People come to see Lawrence, obviously, but Scott manages the kitchen, the menus, all that stuff."

"Does Scott mind that Lawrence takes all the credit?" Charlotte asked, intrigued.

For a moment, Cressida looked confused. "I-I... Well, I've never thought about it like that. We pay Scott well above the average for someone in his position." She shook her head a little, as if dismissing the thought. "No, Scott's fine."

"When did you notice Lawrence had gone?" Angus asked.

"When he didn't turn up for the first sitting on Tuesday. I tried calling, but his phone was off. That wasn't unusual. He often let it run out of charge. Like I said, he doesn't like technology and only had a phone because I insisted."

There was a pause, then Angus asked, "You said earlier that you didn't think he'd come to any harm. Why is that?"

"He visited our London flat the day after he went AWOL. We have one of those doorbell camera things, and it sends an alert whenever anyone goes in or out. He went in, and I had an alert twenty-four hours later that he'd left. I haven't seen him since."

"I'll need the exact times. Have you got the footage?"

Cressida unlocked her tablet computer and opened the doorbell app. She searched the footage for the part where Lawrence was on camera. It was clearly him going into the flat. The next morning, he left the building. Angus noted the timestamps of the footage.

"Is there anyone in London he might have seen? Any reason why he would go there?"

"I have no idea. We have lots of friends in London, though."

"Have you contacted any of them?"

"Don't be silly – I can't go asking all our friends if they've seen Lawrence. It would take for ever. Besides, we're not *that* close to most of them, and one might spill the beans to the media." She thought for a moment. "You could try his TV producer. He went to see her a few weeks before. Maybe he went back."

Charlotte leaned forward, resting her elbows on the table. "Was there anything in his behaviour that made you think he wasn't coping? Or a behaviour pattern similar to the last time he went missing?"

"I didn't notice anything. I mean, the last time, he'd been drinking a bit more than usual, but Lawrence likes a drink. Always has done."

Angus's face grew serious. "I have to ask this next question, I'm afraid. Has he ever tried to take his own life?"

Cressida gave a sort of laugh. "No!"

"Has he ever spoken about wanting to take his own life?"

"No," she said firmly. "He knows the kids would never forgive him." She paused, as if gathering her thoughts.

13

"Sophie is seventeen and Rufus is eighteen. They're both at private school in Cheshire."

"Have you asked them if they've heard from their dad?"

"They haven't. Anyway, Lawrence doesn't contact them in term time. He leaves that to me." She paused. "He's never been an affectionate father. But he's always provided for them, and their school is one of the best in the country."

That sounded lonely to Charlotte, though presumably the children had each other. If a child was away most of the year, their school was effectively doing the parenting. She was glad she hadn't made her fortune before her two sons had gone through state school.

"You will start straight away, won't you?" Cressida asked.

Angus paused a moment, then added. "Yes."

Chapter Three

C harlotte and Angus walked back towards the car park. Once they were a good distance away from Oceanique, Charlotte stopped and leaned against the seafront railings. "What do you think about all that?"

Angus stopped too. "I'm surprised Lawrence Westwood is having issues like that. I mean, on his TV show, he doesn't seem highly strung. Just passionate about food."

Charlotte ran her hand along the cold metal, looking at nothing in particular. "They wouldn't broadcast anything that highlighted his personal problems."

"True."

"So what do we do first?" Charlotte asked. "Back to the bat cave?"

Angus put his hand on his stomach. "How about fish and chips first? I'm starving. Then we can visit the skipper of Lawrence's boat."

Charlotte clapped her hands together. "Fantastic idea – I haven't had fish and chips for ages! We passed one on the way here. I'm buying."

When they reached the fish and chip shop, Angus

waited for Charlotte on a bench looking out over the estuary. He read through his notes from the meeting. Missing persons had been a common feature of his time in the police. His first case with Charlotte had been a missing person too. He'd needed her help with the technical stuff, and she'd proved herself invaluable. And just as in that case, there wasn't much to go on. If only Lawrence was more reliant on computers and phones.

His phone pinged with a message from Jo. They'd been on a date to Okehampton the week before. Not the most exciting of places, but the pub they'd visited had been nice and the food excellent.

Jo had worked as bar staff for years, and before that, in retail. She was intelligent and thoughtful, but he couldn't help comparing her to Charlotte, though he didn't want to.

Jo wasn't unpredictable and impulsive. She was steady. Yes, that was a good word to describe her: steady. Steady was what Rhona, his ex-wife, had been.

So one date was all they'd had so far, and now she'd texted asking if he wanted to meet up again.

He saw Charlotte approaching, laden with food, and put his phone away. He'd answer Jo later.

Charlotte sat down next to him and handed him one of the paper packages. Then she delved into her pocket and pulled out a small bottle of malt vinegar. She sprinkled some over the fish and chips, then offered it to Angus.

He took it, unwrapped his own bundle and did the same.

Meanwhile, Charlotte pulled out a small squeezy bottle of ketchup.

Angus gave her an amused glance. "Did you buy those from the chippy?"

Charlotte popped a chip in her mouth. "No, I brought

them from home. I fancied a trip to the chippy, but they only have those really annoying little sachets."

Angus chuckled. "You have to use your teeth to open them. Complete waste of plastic."

"Exactly! I've got proper forks too." She delved into her handbag and pulled out a plastic bag with two steel forks.

"You really were prepared!" Angus took one of the forks.

"I wasn't leaving Exmouth without fish and chips! You suggested it just before I was going to."

They sat eating in silence, looking at Dawlish Warren on the other side of the river: a nature reserve with a long, sandy beach. Angus wondered why he'd never gone there on the Starcross ferry from Exmouth. Maybe he'd come back at the weekend and try it. He'd always liked going on boats. When they went on family holidays he'd always dragged Rhona and their daughter, Grace, onto any boat or ferry.

"I can't believe the summer we're having. It feels like we're abroad," Charlotte commented between mouthfuls. She took a deep sniff of her bundle of food. "God, I love the smell of fish and chips. It's almost as good as eating them."

"I'll need you to run your usual checks on the internet and dark Web as soon as we get back."

"It might take longer, seeing as he's a celebrity. There'll be extra stuff to look through and filter out. He's been in the news quite a lot over the years."

"Was he the chef who got caught stealing luxury goods from a supermarket?" Angus asked.

Charlotte shook her head. "No, that was Miles Fisher. He gets a thrill from stealing when he uses the self-service tills, even though he's worth millions."

"Haven't seen him on the TV lately."

"I never liked him." Charlotte screwed up her nose. "Too thin. No chef should be thin: that's suspicious."

Angus nodded. "That is a very astute observation and true, now you mention it."

"Cressida seemed very concerned about the business, but not that Lawrence was missing." Charlotte ate another chip and ruminated. "There was no sign of her wanting him back because she missed him."

A seagull swooped down and landed on the pavement in front of them, hoping for a treat.

"Yes, I noticed that too." Angus shooed away the bird. "Go on, be off with you."

"Lots of people stay in a relationship even when the love's gone. I still wonder if Idris had fallen out of love with me before he started his affair with Michelle. Maybe he hadn't loved me for years."

"Did you ask him?"

"No. My therapist said I shouldn't ask. Misty says it's better not to know."

"She may be right."

"How long were you married to Rhona before you realised you weren't in love with her?"

Angus thought. "I still love her, but not like that. It's a friendship love now, rather than partnership love."

Charlotte picked up a piece of battered fish, dipped it in ketchup and took a bite. A fishing boat glided out from the docks. "Have you ever been on a fishing boat? I haven't: I get terrible seasickness."

Angus knew: Woody, her older brother, had told him not so long ago. Charlotte's billionaire friend with benefits, Ross, had bought her a speedboat for her birthday and she hadn't been able to use it.

"I went out a few times when I was a child, with my dad

and Duncan, but I haven't been in years. Might have to rectify that."

"Feeling the lure of the sea?"

"Maybe. Anyway, don't you go on expensive yachts with the other multimillionaires?"

"No. Like I said, I get seasick even on those great big things."

"Have you tried a cruise ship?"

"I went on a big ferry from Dover to Calais when I was teenager and I threw up the whole time. I don't think a boat or ship exists that won't make me seasick." Charlotte scrunched up her fish-and-chip paper and turned to Angus. "Ready when you are."

"You eat too quickly." Angus still had a third of his food left.

When Angus had finished eating, they walked along the seafront to Exmouth quay. Its mix of old and modern buildings was charming, but they weren't there to shop or admire. It was time to find Remy, the skipper of Lawrence's boat.

Chapter Four

Boats of different sizes bobbed gently in the marina, from small fishing vessels to larger leisure craft, all set against the backdrop of the Exe Estuary. The gentle clinking of rigging hardware on the masts, combined with the murmur of locals and tourists, formed the soundtrack of this quintessential Devon harbour.

It didn't take Charlotte and Angus long to find Lawrence's boat, *Bistro Buoy*. A larger than average fishing vessel, painted a vibrant shade of green, it was equipped with large net booms on each side. The deck was lined with neatly arranged lobster pots.

"Hello!" Angus called from the quayside. The man on the boat, who was coiling some ropes, looked up. "Remy Le Gall?"

"Oui," the man replied in a thick French accent. He was in his thirties with sandy-blond hair, a deep tan and wore a T-shirt and shorts.

"Êtes-vous français?" Angus asked without thinking.

Charlotte suppressed a smile. She loved it when Angus spoke French.

"Oui."

"Nous travaillons pour Cressida. Elle cherche son mari, Lawrence. Pourrions-nous monter à bord et vous parler pendant quelques minutes, s'il vous plaît?"

Remy raised his eyebrows. Charlotte wasn't sure whether it was because of what Angus had asked, or surprise at how good his French was.

Eventually, Remy beckoned for them to come aboard. "Did you ask if we could come aboard for a chat?" Charlotte whispered.

Angus nodded.

"Excellent. Don't mind me: carry on speaking in French as much as you like." She smirked.

"Are you staying there?" Angus asked.

"Oh no. I'm fine in port, and when a boat is tied up. Just don't take me out there." She pointed out to sea.

They crossed the gangplank and Remy shook hands with Angus. "'Ow can I 'elp?"

Charlotte looked about her warily.

"You okay?" asked Angus.

She managed a smile. Maybe boarding a boat just after stuffing her face with fish and chips hadn't been such a good idea. "Yup, no problem."

Angus turned to Remy. "Can you tell me when you last saw Lawrence?"

Remy let out a sigh. "I dunno. A week ago, maybe. We don't see each other much."

"Can you remember the exact day? It's important."

Remy took out a packet of cigarettes, lit one and took a long drag. "Last Thursday."

"You haven't seen him after that?"

"Non."

"And when you saw him, did he mention any unusual plans or changes in routine?"

"Non. He discussed the change in seasons and what seafood we should catch for the restaurant."

"And does the whole catch go to the restaurant?"

"Most. If there is extra, it is sold at Brixham Fish Market."

"How much hand does Lawrence have in how the boat is run?"

"Hand?" Remy looked at his own hand, puzzled.

"Sorry, er, est-ce que Lawrence interfère avec votre travail sur le bateau?"

"Ah. Your French iz very good. Lawrence, he leave me alone to run ze boat."

"Did he seem worried or anxious about anything?"

"Non. Rien."

Charlotte wandered along the deck as Angus spoke to Remy, and peered through the window to the cabin. She placed her palm on the window with a thud which made them both look round. "I get terrible seasickness," she said, pushing her hair off her face with her other hand. I know we're moored, but I need to sit down. Is there somewhere?"

Remy nodded. "In bridge. Just don't touch anyzing."

"Thanks," she said. She walked warily inside and out of sight.

"How many do you have on the crew here?"

"Three in summer, when zere are more fish to catch."

"Would it be possible to speak to them, to see if they know where Lawrence might be?"

"Non. They are all away for a few days. Zey never talk to him anyway. Lawrence, he just talk to me."

"Are there any areas nearby where Lawrence liked to

fish or relax? Anywhere quiet, not well known? A quiet bay somewhere?"

"You mean, did he take the boat to hide somewhere? Non. He did not use the boat. Only I have ze keys. I am ze captain."

"All right. Thank you for your time. If you see Lawrence, or find out anything about his location, please contact me straight away." Angus took out a business card and handed it to Remy. "I'd better retrieve my colleague." He walked up to the bridge and peered in.

Charlotte was sitting on the captain's chair, which was a cross between an office chair and a dodgy 1980s' armchair. She appeared engrossed in her phone.

"Charlotte, I'm ready to go."

Charlotte looked up from her phone and smiled. "I'm ready to go too."

Once they were a safe distance from the boat, Angus turned to Charlotte. "Were you hacking into the boat's computer?"

Charlotte grinned. "I could see from the computer display in the bridge that he's just got back from France."

"France? Well, he is French. Maybe he lives there or visits. Where in France did he go?"

"Perros-Guirec."

"I don't know it."

Charlotte stopped, took out her phone, opened a map app and typed in the name. "Here you are: a small coastal town in Brittany." She handed the phone to Angus.

"It looks pretty similar to Exmouth," he commented. "Unremarkable, but almost exactly due south of here."

"I'll see what I can find out about it."

They started walking again. "You didn't see it on the display, did you?" He narrowed his eyes. "You hacked it."

"No, really I didn't. It was on the display. I took some photos of it: that's what I was doing with my phone." She showed Angus her photos of the computer display.

"All right, I believe you. It might be nothing, but we'll add it as our first piece of potentially useful information."

Chapter Five

Charlotte sat back in her study chair and scanned the computer screen in front of her.

Her search for information about Lawrence on the internet and the dark Web had uncovered tabloid articles, gossip, fan praise, haters, and even spoof comedy sketches by fans on TikTok.

"Apparently, Lawrence is in the process of writing his autobiography," she told Angus, who was sitting across from her in her study, going over the list of friends and family which Cressida had given them. "I've never been a fan of celebrity memoirs. They always have so-called humorous titles based on something tenuous. And a big retouched photo of the celebrity on the cover. Most of them are just boring. Actors, or people on reality shows who've became famous for being famous."

Angus looked up. "He won't be writing it, though. They're all written by a ghostwriter who interviews the celebrity."

"That's cheating."

Angus shrugged. "Plenty of authors use ghostwriters."

"Then they're not authors."

"It sells books, though. Put a famous person's name on the book and it's much more likely to fly off the shelves."

"That's very unfair to real authors."

"Indeed. Anything else about Lawrence?"

"He got a lot of hate on social media for criticising vegan synthetic-meat products."

Angus puffed out a breath. "That's not a good idea, having a go at vegans."

"I know. He got a lot of hate, but a lot of support too. Anyway, he doubled down. He took photos of himself eating meat and posted them on social media." Charlotte smiled. "Actually, I'm starting to like him."

"You don't like vegans?"

"No, I just don't like the militant ones who think they have the right to tell everyone else what they can and can't eat."

"Anything else?" Angus asked, changing the subject.

"Nothing much. Just the new season of his TV show out in a few months, and a few minor articles about his charitable efforts to help people using foodbanks make better meals."

"Sounds like a good cause," Angus commented.

"To be honest, there's so much about him that it could take ages to find anything relevant to our case."

Charlotte walked over to the other side of the study and pulled out the blank conspiracy board and placed it on the sideboard ready to be filled in. "So who is on Cressida's list of names and addresses?"

Angus picked up the A4 sheet. "Twelve people, all friends or business acquaintances. She's given brief information about each of them and their contact details. Top of the list is a woman called Liz Morgan with two asterisks next to her name. That means Cressida has called her."

Charlotte pondered. "Don't you think it's strange that she hasn't called all of them?"

"I was just thinking that."

"You'd think she'd be more panicked by him being missing all this time. Do you think we should notify the police?"

"I've considered it, but no, not yet. Cressida asked us not to, and I can't see any reason why we should. But I will if I think there's been any kind of foul play."

"I think we should visit the places he went last time and then the London property, especially as we know he went there. He might still be in London."

"He'll be difficult to find if so."

Charlotte tapped the pen against her lips. "Not if you're in the police. There are so many CCTV cameras in London that you can be tracked everywhere."

"We don't have access to them all, though."

"Shame," she said, with a knowing smile.

"We'll go to the glamping site in Wales first."

"Tonight or tomorrow?"

Angus looked at his watch. "It's only two o'clock: we could be in Wales by three thirty. The site is in Builth Wells. I'll text you the address."

Charlotte's phone pinged and she brought the place up on a map. "The roads leading there are pretty narrow and ropey. I don't think the Bentley would survive them. I should get a four-by-four. Do you think it would be helpful?"

"We'll go in my car," Angus said. His black VW Golf was inconspicuous and reliable.

"The glamping site is on a farm. They have two luxury

yurts on a Welsh hillside." Charlotte tapped a few keys and the glamping website appeared. "Two hundred and fifty pounds a night per yurt. Looks lovely, actually. You have a proper bed, and there's a kitchen next to the yurt, as well as a bathroom, sauna and shower."

Angus came over and looked. "Looks nice. Pricey, though."

"Have you ever stayed in a yurt?"

Angus shook his head. "No. I might change my mind when I see it, but at my age, I'm not keen on camping."

"This is glamping, though. A whole different kettle of fish."

"You tempted?"

Charlotte laughed. "Certainly not. I only want proper hotels. Preferably with a spa."

Twenty minutes later, they were in Angus's VW Golf, heading up the M5 motorway towards Wales.

Chapter Six

They were still a few miles from the glamping site when the road became single track and rough. The trees lining the road got thicker the farther they went.

Angus's VW Golf handled the road well, and it was only when he turned into the farm lane that the road surface got even worse.

"What is it with farms and their lack of decent roads?" Charlotte asked.

Angus shrugged. "If you're in a tractor or four-by-four, repairing the roads probably isn't your highest priority."

The farmhouse was hidden by tall trees which looked as if they hadn't been cut back in decades. Between two of them was a gate with a sign: Afon Wye Farm.

Angus stopped the car and turned off the engine. "They aren't exactly keen on letting the glampers know where to go. No signs anywhere."

Charlotte looked at her phone. "The website doesn't say how to find the yurts. I guess we can call at the farmhouse and find out if Lawrence is here."

They walked through the gate and the farmhouse became visible: a white-rendered building which looked at least a few hundred years old. The windows were single-glazed, the paint peeling from the frames.

"That looks like a back door," Angus commented, pointing at a sturdy white door with no bell or knocker.

"Bit strange, isn't it? You'd think they'd make it as easy as possible for holidaymakers to find out where to go. If I ran a holiday let, I'd do everything possible to make sure the punters weren't put off."

"It's a secluded place. Maybe they want it to remain that way."

Charlotte studied Angus. "You know, we've been working together over a year now, and your only holiday during that time has been visiting family in Scotland. Do you ever go away?"

Angus pushed his glasses up his nose. "I do. Just not recently."

"You should book somewhere and take a break. Where do you usually go?"

"Greece, Spain, Canary Islands. Rhona always picked. She liked to sunbathe and relax by the pool."

"You don't strike me as the kind of man who'd enjoy that."

He shrugged. "I didn't mind. When I was in the police, I needed the time to stop and do nothing. But since then—"

Charlotte interrupted him. "Since then, you've not been on holiday at all."

"I've been too busy."

"All work and no holiday isn't good for anyone. I'm planning on going to the Cayman Islands in a few months. Why don't you come with me? Ross has been and said it was amazing. Miles of golden beaches, and amazing wildlife."

"The Caymans?"

"Yep."

Angus gave a small laugh. "You're serious?"

"Of course I am. I'll take a scheduled flight, but I'll be going first class."

"I don't doubt it."

"Come on, it'll be fun. Look at it as a way of saying thank you for saving me from wallowing in self-pity."

"Haven't you got a friend to go with?"

"Yes. You."

Angus thought about spending time with Charlotte away from Exeter, Devon and work. He needed a holiday, and he knew enough about the Cayman Islands to know it would be the holiday of a lifetime and like no other he'd had. Maybe going away together would change their relationship into something more meaningful. But then, she'd just called him a friend.

As Angus opened his mouth to answer, his phone beeped. It was a text, from his mother:

Hello love, just a quick message to say we're on a little adventure in the camper van. Mum x

Charlotte put her head to one side. "Anything interesting?"

Angus put his phone back in his pocket. "Just my mum. Nothing important."

Angus knocked on the door of the farmhouse. There was no response.

"I was expecting to hear dogs barking," Charlotte commented. "People with farms always have dogs."

Angus knocked again. After a minute or two, he started

31

to walk towards the side of the house. As he reached the corner, the door opened. "Can I help you?" said a woman of about sixty. She was dressed in jeans, a thick green woolly jumper and green wellies.

"Liz Morgan?"

"Yes." Liz looked from Angus to Charlotte.

"We're working for Cressida Westwood. We're looking for Lawrence."

Liz frowned. "Lawrence? What would he be doing here?"

"Can we come in?" Angus asked.

"I was about to feed the pigs. You can come along." She looked down at their footwear. "Don't worry, there's not been any rain recently." She stepped out and closed the door behind her.

"So Cressida's lost Lawrence again, has she?" Liz asked, as she led them around the farmhouse. Her tone was light, sarcastic even.

"I'm afraid so," Angus replied. "Have you seen him?"

"Not for a year. So Cressida told you he came here before?"

"Yes." Angus said.

"Well, if he's run away from her again, he hasn't come here. That makes sense, though. If he wants to get away from her, going to the same place twice is a stupid idea."

"What do you mean?"

"Hopefully he's ditched Cressida for good this time. She's no good for him."

They walked to a small shed. Liz lifted the latch, went inside and brought out a large black bucket filled with food scraps and pellets. Then she took them to the pigpen, a large enclosure with a metal sty, surrounded by a wooden fence. Inside were three black pigs.

Liz rattled the bucket and the pigs charged over.

She climbed the fence and the three pigs grunted and snorted loudly, following Liz to the trough where she poured out the food. She patted one of them on the back, then returned to Angus and Charlotte. "I've only got these three now," she said. "I had a dozen a couple of years ago and I sold the meat, but now I just eat them myself." The pigs were hoovering up the food alarmingly fast.

They all stood watching for a moment. "How did you and Lawrence get to know each other?" Angus asked.

"We were at university together, studying law. It never suited Lawrence: he only did the degree to please his parents. As soon as he graduated, he went into cooking. Sorry, cheffing. Never saw that coming, but we lived in halls that provided our meals. I never thought he was interested in food."

Charlotte gave a small nod of her head, her interest piqued. She hadn't discovered that fact about Lawrence in her internet research. "I had no idea he had a law degree."

"I know. He keeps it quiet. He's not ashamed of it – he just wanted to move on. After he graduated, he confided in me and told me all he'd ever wanted to do was cook. When he first started, though, he was terrible. It took him five years training in France before he came back a decent chef."

"Has he contacted you recently?" Angus asked.

Liz glanced at Angus. "We message each other on Facebook sometimes, but not often. We're both busy people. And our friendship is the sort where it doesn't matter if we don't contact each other; we're still good friends. So long as I don't have to see Cressida, I'm fine."

"Why the dislike of Cressida?"

Liz gave a sardonic laugh. "We just don't get on. She's not good for him. She's the brains behind his empire, that's for sure. She's the one who approached TV companies to get him on the box. She's the one who got him a literary agent and pushed for his book deals. All he ever wanted to do was be the best chef in England, then the UK, then the world. But Cressida's only interested in the money. That's why she wants him back. Not because she cares about him, but because she needs him for her next scheme," Liz huffed in disapproval. "I wouldn't be surprised if she was siphoning off cash for herself."

Angus and Charlotte glanced at each other. "Do you have any proof of that?" Angus asked.

Liz grinned. "None at all. But I know them both."

"Cressida told us that she is struggling to keep the restaurant going without Lawrence," Angus stated. "She needs him to run the kitchen."

Liz harrumphed and folded her arms.

The only sound was the pigs snuffling at the empty trough. Angus took out his notebook and turned a few pages. "Do you know where he is?"

"Me?" She laughed, "No, I don't. And before you ask, no, he hasn't contacted me, or told me he's run away again. But I wish he had. I'd help him any way I could."

"So you don't know why he might have disappeared? He hasn't mentioned any mental health issues or other problems?"

"Only Cressida."

Angus searched for a way to keep the conversation going. "Do you get booked out with the yurts?"

"In the summer holidays, yes, and at Easter. Not so much outside those times, but we get enough profit to justify keeping them going."

"Mind if I take a look around one?"

"Of course you can."

She led them through a gate to another field. The yurts were at opposite ends. In the middle was a timber bathroom block. Next to each yurt was a small wooden kitchen block, and a little farther away, a composting toilet.

"Are you considering a holiday in one of these?" Charlotte whispered, when Liz was too far away to hear.

"Just wanted to see if there were any guests staying," Angus whispered back. "If you get my drift."

Liz came over, her face full of enthusiasm. "The yurts are fantastic: they stand up to everything the Welsh weather can throw at them. We pack them away for winter, though: we don't get enough people to keep them up all year."

"It's high up here," Charlotte said. "Do you get snow in winter?"

"Yes, and the rain can be relentless. We put them up in March and start taking guests shortly after."

"How long does it take to put the yurts up?"

"About a day."

"It looks lovely and peaceful."

"It is. Apart from anything else, the mobile signal here is almost non existent. And if they want to charge their phone or devices, they have to come to the farmhouse."

Charlotte's eyebrows shot up. "There's no electricity?"

"Nope. It's truly off grid. Lots of people come here to detox from social media and computer use." Angus watched Charlotte, but she didn't flinch. "Do you want to look inside one?"

They entered the nearest yurt. A spacious wooden bed with a patterned bedspread sat in the middle, and to the side were rustic furnishings: a wicker bedside table and a simple wooden chair. The yurt's wooden lattices met at the peak of the canvas ceiling, allowing natural light to fill the space with a soft glow. Traditional rugs added warmth and a splash of colour to the yurt's cosy, bohemian vibe.

Angus took it all in. "Very nice."

"It looks much nicer in real life," Charlotte agreed.

"I designed the interior myself," said Liz. "The other yurt has different patterns and colours, but the ambience is still bohemian."

"Are they booked this week?"

"I've got a couple arriving tomorrow, and then a few other bookings this month."

Liz showed them the bathroom block and then accompanied them to their car.

"If Lawrence contacts you, please let us know." Angus handed Liz his card.

She glanced at it. "I doubt he will. But I'll tell him to get himself home if he does. I expect his children will want to see him."

Once they were on their way back to Devon in Angus's car, they discussed the visit.

"I thought you were about to book a holiday there," Charlotte said, with a smile.

Angus glanced at her. "No, I just wanted to see if she was resistant to showing us the yurts. If Lawrence was staying in one, there's no way she would have let us near them."

"Did you think she was lying, then?"

"I needed to be sure. Her reaction to Lawrence missing seemed natural."

"He could have been in the house," Charlotte said.

"Yes. That's a possibility, but I don't think he is."

Charlotte mulled this over. "I could find a reason to go back and take a look around."

Angus raised an eyebrow. "You mean hack her Wi-Fi."

"Absolutely not." Angus's eyebrow climbed a little higher. "Apart from anything else, she doesn't have Wi-Fi. I checked. She must use her phone data to access the internet."

Chapter Seven

Angus dropped Charlotte home, then headed to his semi-detached house in the Pennsylvania area of Exeter. Charlotte was going to continue her internet and dark Web searches, in hopes of finding some information about Lawrence's whereabouts.

Angus decided to go for a run before dinner. That would clear his head and help him plan what to do next. They would need to visit London and the Westwoods' flat soon. Perhaps Lawrence would have left a clue as to where he'd gone.

When Angus turned into his road, the view of his house was blocked by an enormous camper van on his drive. "What the—"

The camper van's door opened and a man stepped out. He was tall and bulky, in his mid-seventies, silver-haired, and wearing shorts and a T-shirt. *Dad.*

Angus's father saw his car approaching and waved. Angus parked on the road, got out, and was immediately engulfed by a hug that lifted him off the ground.

Gordon Darrow was about twice the size of Angus in

width, and at least a few inches taller. "Good to see ya, son," he said, in his strong Scottish accent. He held Angus by the shoulders, looking at him.

"You too, Dad. Is Mum in there?"

"She is! Come on out, Eileen. Angus is here."

Angus looked at the door. "What are you doing here? Have you driven all the way from Stirling?"

"Aye. We wanted to come to the Sidmouth Folk Festival again. It's been years since we've been and we're not getting any younger, so we thought we'd come doon. But your mum didnae want to sleep in a tent." He chuckled. "Not at her age. Besides, this has everything we need. Kitchen, bathroom, bed, TV. I'll give you a tour later. The sides expand, you see, and it doubles in size."

"Is that you, Angus?" His mum appeared in the doorway and smiled. In her early seventies, she still had a youthful spark in her eyes, her soft silver hair framing her face. She hadn't changed much since he'd last seen her, at Christmas.

"Hi, Mum. You're a sight for sore eyes."

She came to meet him and they hugged. "It's good to see you, Mum."

She looked into his face. "You look well. How have you been? Are you still single? Have you not found a nice lady to take care of you?"

Angus chuckled. "Not yet."

She continued, "We've not heard from Rhona lately. But I suppose if you two are officially divorced now, she'll have divorced us too."

"I think she's been busy," Angus said. "She's taken on more responsibility at the council and it's eating up all her time. That's what Grace says, anyway."

"Did you tell him he needs to have a look inside?"

Eileen asked her husband. She turned back to Angus. "It's very fancy, you know. Come on in and look, son. You'll love it. When you see it, you'll want one of your own."

Angus had never seen the appeal of camper vans, but his father shepherded him inside. It was even bigger than he had expected.

Gordon waved a hand at their surroundings. "This is the kitchen. It's got an oven, but these days we use the air fryer most of the time. The bathroom's over there. It's got a shower, toilet and sink. The water tank holds enough for four showers. The bed's up there." He pointed to a sort of shelf above the kitchen with a retractable ladder.

"Are you sure you're both okay climbing up there at night?" He wasn't sure they should be climbing ladders at their age.

"Did you hear that, Eileen? He thinks we're too old to climb a ladder." Gordon chuckled.

Angus rolled his eyes. "I didn't mean it like that. I just want you to be careful."

They looked at each other and Gordon smiled. "Aye, ye did. But we'd rather you worry about us than not. We're glad for your concern, son."

Angus's phone pinged: a text had arrived.

"We've not come at a bad time, have we?" his mother asked, concerned.

"What? No, of course not. You're always welcome. I mean, I'm on a case, but I've always got time for my two favourite parents. Come inside and we'll catch up properly. When are you going to the folk festival?"

"They open the campsite tomorrow," said his father. "We'll head over about lunchtime, and the festival starts on Friday."

In his kitchen, Angus put the kettle on and sneaked a

look at his phone. It was what he'd expected: a message from Charlotte.

Just found something interesting about Lawrence on the dark Web. Apparently, he's been mistaken for a Mexican soap-opera star. There's even a fan page dedicated to Lawrence. He's also got fans analysing his three-second appearance in the background of a cult sci-fi film.

"You *have* got a lady friend," said his father, from over his shoulder.

Angus whipped the phone away like a teenager caught with a copy of *Playboy*. "She's my work colleague," he said, quickly.

His dad chuckled. "'Course she is, son." He walked off.

Angus took out his phone again. *Can't really talk, parents here.*

Charlotte replied: *What, from Scotland? You didn't tell me they were visiting!* A sad-face emoji followed.

They didn't tell me they were coming. It was a surprise.

Charlotte didn't reply. Presumably, that meant she was satisfied.

Angus went into the living room with the tea. Half an hour later, they were deep in conversation about his brother, Duncan, and nephew, Ewan, when the doorbell rang.

For a split second, Angus wondered who it might be, then remembered that Charlotte hadn't replied to his last message. He'd bet a large sum of money that when he opened the door, Charlotte would be standing there.

As he'd predicted, when he opened the door, she didn't wait to be asked in. "Hello, Angus! I thought I'd drop in and say hi to your parents. Don't worry, I won't stay long."

He should have been annoyed at her for just turning up without warning. In fact, a few months ago, he would have been. But just turning up was one of the things that Charlotte did. And he liked that about her.

* * *

Charlotte walked past him and went into the living room, then made a beeline for his mother.

"Hello, I'm Charlotte." She held out her hand and his mother shook it.

Then she turned to his father, who ignored her hand and engulfed her in a hug which almost lifted her off the floor. "I'm very pleased to meet you, lassie! You're the one who helped Ewan, aren't ye?"

"Oh, are you that Charlotte?" his mother asked. Gordon let her go.

"Yes! How is Ewan? Is he enjoying his apprenticeship?"

"Oh, aye," Angus's father said. "He loves it: he's like a new boy. You worked a miracle with him. We were all worried for a while."

"You did, and we're so grateful," Eileen said.

"That's very kind of you, but I didn't come here for praise and thanks. I wanted to meet you both. Angus has told me all about you."

"Has he, now?" Gordon said, with a laugh. "All good, I hope."

"Of course," Charlotte said, slightly nervously.

"Let's sit down and we can have a chat. Can you stay for a wee drink?"

"Er, I don't really drink much these days, but I'll stay for a chat."

"I'll make you a cup of tea," Angus said, and went to the kitchen.

Gordon pointed to the settee. "Come and sit down."

Charlotte did as she was told. "So you've come in the motorhome outside?"

"Aye, we have," Eileen said. "We're only renting it, but if we get on with it, we might buy one and go on more adventures. Maybe even to Europe."

"I like that we can go wherever we want," said Gordon. "Eileen here says it's more comfortable than our house!"

Eileen laughed. "He's exaggerating, of course, but it is a lovely way to see the country. You must take a tour of it before we leave. Maybe you could even join us for a day at the folk festival? That's why we're here."

Charlotte considered this. Angus had mentioned that his parents used to drag him along to Sidmouth Folk Festival when he was a child. He'd also said that he'd like to go again. Maybe it wasn't such a bad idea. "I might take you up on that. It sounds like a great festival. What do you like best about it?"

"I like the ceilidhs, and Gordon plays fiddle, so we keep ourselves busy. We've got enough stories from the festival to keep us up all night. Right, Gordon?"

"Indeed we do. But let's save some for later. You'll stay for dinner, won't you, Charlotte?"

"As long as I'm not intruding..."

"Not at all! Angus has been much happier since you've been around. It's a relief for a mother to see her son doing well."

Charlotte felt her cheeks heat up. "Thank you. Angus is... He's been great to work with. We make a good team. I have two sons myself. You never stop worrying about them, do you?"

Gordon leaned forward, his expression more serious. "He's told us about some of your cases, and it sounds like you two have been through quite a lot. You're not just good for him professionally. He needs people who understand him, who see the world the way he does."

"And it's nice to see him so passionate about his work again," Eileen added. "He was in a tough spot for a while before he left the police, but we've noticed a change since he partnered with you."

Charlotte smiled, touched by their words. "We've got each other's backs, and that's important in our line of work."

Gordon smiled approvingly.

Chapter Eight

"Okay, where next?" Charlotte said, the next morning. The weather was clear and bright, and the forecast predicted a warm day. She took a bite of her toast and moaned in appreciation.

Angus screwed his face up. "What is on that toast?"

"Peanut butter and Marmite."

"I thought so. That's disgusting."

"Not to me. I love peanut butter and I love Marmite, can't think of anything better." She took a huge bite of the toast, smiling.

Angus frowned. "Did you make that yourself?"

"The toast? Yes. That is my limit, though."

"You didn't burn it. I'm impressed."

"Growth mindset," Charlotte said, and smiled. "It's not just about digital skills. Although I won't be attempting cordon bleu. I did watch a few of Lawrence's cooking videos, though. He cooked Super Speedy Butter Chicken in twenty minutes, but only a trained chef could chop veggies that fast, and the sauce was incredibly unhealthy. Lots of butter and cream."

"You're not a fan, then."

"I didn't say that. Just that he's fast at cooking because it's his profession. Not everyone can be."

Angus put his hands in his pockets and sat on the edge and leaned against the kitchen counter. "I watched an episode of his UK travel show last night and I enjoyed it. He was in Shetland and he cooked some local dishes."

"Yes, he's travelling around for this new series, but earlier ones were in a studio."

"So we should visit Lawrence's TV producer in London."

It was Charlotte's turn to screw up her face. "Ugh, not London! I hate it there."

"Really? Didn't you grow up nearby?"

"Near it, yes. Not in it. Hemel Hempstead is about half an hour away on the train. Commuter distance."

"We should be in and out quickly enough. Why don't you like London?"

"Too many people. I prefer Devon." Charlotte's eyes narrowed. "I don't remember you ever going to London."

Angus considered. "Haven't been for a few years. Last time I went was for a weekend, with Malcolm. We went to watch the London Marathon."

"Weren't you tempted to run it yourself?"

Angus shook his head. "I've thought about it, but there are plenty of runs in Devon. There's the Axe to Exe: I might do that. It's twenty-two miles, so it's close to a marathon."

"It's hard to get a place anyway. In the London Marathon, I mean. My running club has a few places for the marathon every year, so that probably wouldn't be an issue if I really wanted to run it."

Charlotte went through to her study and sat at her desk and tapped the keyboard. "Can't you hack the thousands of

CCTV cameras the councils have?" Angus said, with a laugh.

Charlotte shook her head. "I won't go near those. If it's a private camera, that's different. I'll get Grigore to drive us in the Bentley."

"If we go by train from Exeter, we'll be there in a couple of hours."

Charlotte grimaced. "I hate public transport. Besides, Grigore has been moaning that I haven't been on any long trips recently. This will cheer him up." Charlotte popped the rest of the toast in her mouth.

Angus considered arguing the point, but he wasn't in the mood to fight his corner. The Bentley was comfortable, and they wouldn't be bound by train times. "All right, but we need to leave soon."

"Did your parents get off okay this morning?"

"They did. Oh, and they're insisting we both go to at least one day of the festival. Saturday has the most going on. The rest of the week is still busy, but it's more workshops and gigs."

"Saturday works for me. Folk music isn't my thing, but I'm willing to give it a go. Will there be Morris dancers?"

"Yes, lots of them."

"Oh no," she complained.

"I love a bit of Morris! There's nothing so quintessentially English as Morris dancers," Angus stated.

Charlotte grimaced.

He changed the subject. "How did the internet research go?"

"I haven't found anything particularly interesting, but I did discover that Lawrence has a number of accounts with streaming services. He doesn't use social media. While he

47

has accounts on all the major platforms, as Cressida said, someone posts for him."

"All right, what about Liz Morgan? Has anything come up there?"

"There was more about her. She's got an Instagram account which she posts to regularly, but there hasn't been much recently. Most of what she posts is photos from the farm, but I've seen nothing to indicate that Lawrence has visited lately."

Angus sighed. "Well, we'd better get going if we're visiting Lawrence's TV producer in London."

When Charlotte told Grigore that she needed him to drive to London, his eyes lit up. "Car is clean, ready to go when you vant."

Charlotte clapped her hands. "Excellent! Angus is coming too."

The journey would take at least three and a half hours, so Charlotte took her laptop. "Where exactly in London are we going?" she asked, as she opened it.

Angus handed her a small piece of paper. "Cameron Wright, Upper Marsh Street, South Bank," Charlotte read.

"We'll also visit the Westwoods' London flat," Angus said. "I need to see if Lawrence left any clues as to what he was doing in London."

Charlotte nodded, not looking up from her laptop. "I have a question for you."

"Oh yes? What is it?"

"What cybersecurity questions would you have for someone who's starting a podcast?"

"About cybersecurity?"

Charlotte nodded.

Angus looked out at the passing scenery and thought. "I don't know. Why are you asking?"

Charlotte grinned. "I'm starting a podcast!"

Angus turned to face her, eyebrows raised, then a smile slowly spread across his face. "Okaaay..."

Charlotte held his gaze, waiting for his response.

"I don't know. I mean, I have no idea about it, so I don't even know where to start. Have you asked Helena and Grigore?"

"Not yet. I know what you're thinking."

"I doubt that," Angus said.

"You're thinking that everyone's got a podcast these days. Yes, but most of them are about politics, health, and wellness or things like that. Mine will be about helping people avoid getting scammed. The amount of ignorance about cybersecurity is unreal. I want to change that."

Angus's face softened. "A noble cause. And you're right, there is far too much ignorance about cybersecurity."

"It's not people's fault. I mean, the tech has moved on so quickly, it's overwhelming at times."

"And the scammers have caught on quickly."

"Exactly."

"Okay, well, how about explaining what phishing emails are? I get loads of them, and it's hard to tell what's real and what's not."

Charlotte started typing at her laptop. "That's an excellent question."

Chapter Nine

Cameron's office was located in a striking modern building in South Bank, characterised by a sleek glass façade that gleamed under the London sky. The building's design was contemporary, featuring a bold geometric structure and clean lines. Its transparent exterior offered a glimpse into the dynamic world within, while also reflecting the vibrant city life and the Thames flowing nearby.

Grigore pulled up outside and opened the rear door.

"Thanks," Charlotte said, as she got out and looked up at the building. Angus followed her inside.

The lobby was stylish and minimalist. A security guard greeted them, then phoned through, and they were directed to a smart, high-speed elevator. "Third floor," he told them.

As soon as the lift opened, Angus and Charlotte found themselves in a stylish office. Modern, clean lines and lots of glass gave it a calm ambience. On the walls were photos of celebrities and casts from the TV shows which the company produced.

They were met by a man in his fifties, with carefully

styled light-brown hair sprinkled with grey. "Mr Darrow? Cameron Wright." He held out his hand and Angus shook it, then introduced Charlotte. "Come into my office, and we can talk there."

They followed him into a nearby office. Cameron sat behind his desk and Angus and Charlotte sat opposite. Behind him, on the wall, were photos of Cameron smiling with friends. One on a beach somewhere exotic, another on what looked like a yacht.

"So Cressida has lost Lawrence again, has she?" Cameron swung his chair back and forth slightly, amused at Cressida's predicament.

Cameron was the second person so say that Cressida had lost Lawrence again.

Angus nodded. "He's disappeared. She's holding the fort at the restaurant in Exmouth, but she needs him back."

Cameron sat back and gave a heavy sigh. "Honestly, I can't say I blame him. Cressida works him to the bone. She has such a tight hold over him that it's not surprising he's tried to break loose. Do you know how she's pushing him?"

"What do you mean?"

"Cressida wants Lawrence to expand the Exmouth restaurant into a chain of restaurants, even though he wants to stay exclusive. She wants him to do more and more TV shows, but he hates it. We almost dropped Lawrence before the last series: it wasn't good for his mental health, and we could see that. We can't have celebrities with issues, and believe me, Lawrence has issues."

Charlotte's brow furrowed. "I don't understand. I checked the ratings for *Lawrence's Gourmet Adventures*, and it was one of the highest-rated food programmes in the country. People love him. Why wouldn't you want him to film as many shows as possible? I'd have thought a company like yours would do everything to get the most you can out of Lawrence."

Cameron turned to Charlotte and gave her a patronising smile. Until that moment, he'd only spoken to Angus. "Lawrence is one of our most successful presenters, but lately, he's been difficult to work with. That's putting it nicely. We'd almost run out of cameramen to film the show. Three walked away from the series, one after Lawrence had grabbed and threatened him. Cameramen talk to each other, you know. Once word got around that Lawrence was … temperamental, it was almost impossible to find anyone who'd work with him. And that was just the cameramen. His PA was usually in tears in the ladies' toilet."

Angus took out his notebook and started writing.

Cameron raised his eyebrows. "This is all strictly off the record. I thought you knew that."

Angus put away his pen. "Of course. When was the last time you saw Lawrence?"

Cameron sat back in his chair. "There was the time a few months ago, at the wrap party. He got horribly drunk and had to be helped home."

"Has he contacted you lately?"

"He came in a few weeks ago about a production issue: I needed him to come in and redo some of his voice-overs. We had a brief meeting here. Other than that, I haven't seen him."

"He hasn't been back?"

"No. We're not that close, you know. Our relationship is purely professional. If Lawrence was in trouble, I'm not the one he'd go to for help." He spoke in a clipped, offhand tone.

Angus looked at his notes. "How did Lawrence seem when you last saw him?"

Cameron shrugged. "The same as ever. He was fretting

over how the series would be received by the public. He was worried that people weren't watching cookery shows on TV any more, and he said he was going to get on TikTok and YouTube."

"So he was worried about becoming irrelevant to future generations?"

"There seems to be a general fear about missing out on followers online by the presenters. Social media has its place, but TV streaming companies still have more than enough customers from the older generation – and people who don't want to watch everything on a phone or tablet."

"You're not worried, then?"

Cameron sat forward, hands clasped together. "Not at all. Right now, we've been commissioned for more series than ever before."

They were interrupted by a knock at the door. It opened, and a young woman stuck her head into the office. "Sorry to interrupt, Cameron, but you're wanted in the conference room. It's KD: he's worried about the new LA series."

"Thank you, Gemma. I'll be right there."

Gemma closed the door.

"Is there anything else you wanted to know?" Cameron asked.

"Do you know where he might be?" asked Angus.

"In London?"

"Anywhere."

"He has a flat here, but Cressida will have told you that. Otherwise, I have no idea."

Angus looked at Charlotte, who shook her head.

"Well, thank you for seeing us at such short notice. If Lawrence contacts you, please let us know straight away."

Angus delved into his pocket and placed his card on the table.

Cameron eyed it, then picked it up and put it in his desk drawer. Then he stood up. "I'll get Gemma to see you out. I have a meeting."

They walked into the lobby, where Gemma was hovering. "I'll take you to the lift," she said, as Cameron disappeared down the hallway and through a door.

As they stood waiting, Gemma caught Charlotte's eye, then looked sidelong towards the ladies' toilets.

"Er, before we go, could I just use the bathroom?" Charlotte asked.

Gemma pointed. "It's just there."

The lift dinged and the door opened.

"I'll see you downstairs," Angus said, and stepped in.

Charlotte went into the ladies'. A few seconds later, Gemma entered. She checked no one else was in there, then turned to Charlotte. "You're looking for Lawrence, aren't you?" she said in a whisper.

Charlotte nodded. "Yes. How do you know?"

"I overheard Cameron on the phone."

"Do you know where he is?"

"No. But I can tell you that Cameron and Lawrence had a massive argument when he came here a few weeks ago."

"What about?"

Gemma stepped a little closer and lowered her voice. "Cameron's seeing Maxine Dubois."

Charlotte raised her eyebrows. "Am I supposed to know who that is?"

"She's half his age and an up-and-coming chef. She's massive on TikTok. He's planning to get rid of Lawrence and install Maxine as presenter in his place. It's being kept hush-hush at the moment until Lawrence's last show has aired. Then they'll announce it."

"And they had an argument about it?"

"Yeah. Lawrence found out that this series is his last and Max is taking over. Cameron kept him in the dark until the very last minute."

"And he didn't like it, I assume."

"They were both in Cameron's office, shouting. It got really ugly."

"He got violent?"

"God, no. Lawrence isn't like that. But he wasn't happy. He stormed out of Cameron's office, then shouted, 'How could you kick me when I'm down? What am I going to do?'"

"Did you hear anything else?"

"Not really. Just muffled voices, but it all made sense when I overheard her on the phone."

"Why didn't Cameron tell us that Lawrence is being replaced?"

Gemma shrugged. "Like I said, it's all hush-hush at the moment. They want Lawrence's series to finish airing before the announcement."

Charlotte narrowed her eyes. "Why are you telling me this?"

Gemma blinked. "Cameron's a complete bastard. He's always having a go at me for nothing. I'm looking for another job and I can't wait to leave. And Lawrence is lovely. He's always really sweet when he comes in. He even remembers my name. Most people don't: I'm just the office dogsbody."

Charlotte racked her brains for anything else she could ask, but came up with nothing. She looked in her handbag and handed Gemma one of Angus's cards. "This is my partner's number," she said. "Call him if you hear anything else. We need to find Lawrence. If you have any idea where he might be, or if he turns up here, tell us straight away."

Gemma took the card. "I will."

Angus was waiting in the lobby, looking at his phone.

"Hi," Charlotte said. "Sorry I was so long. I have something to tell you."

Angus put his phone in his pocket. "What is it?"

"Let's head outside."

Grigore was parked farther up the road. When he saw Charlotte and Angus, he started the Bentley and pulled up alongside them.

It was only when they were moving off that Charlotte told Angus what Gemma had said.

"So they're ditching Lawrence," Angus mused. "That must have made him even more desperate, especially if Cressida is pressuring him to do more. We need to talk to Cameron again and ask her about her side of the argument. There may be more to it."

"We could go back in," Charlotte said. "Maybe he'll see us when he comes out of his meeting?"

Angus shook his head. "That would make it obvious that Gemma's spilled the beans. We need to give it a bit of time."

"Tomorrow?"

Angus agreed. "We'll visit Lawrence's flat, then head home."

Chapter Ten

Lawrence and Cressida's flat was nestled in the heart of Greenwich, in South East London. Set in an area rich in maritime history, the building was classic Victorian architecture with red brickwork, tall sash windows and ornate stonework. There was a small, well-kept garden in front of the building that added a touch of greenery.

They entered the building through a heavy, carved wooden door. A short flight of stairs led to the first-floor flat. There was a key safe beside the flat's front door, and Angus entered the code given to him by Cressida.

Inside, they walked across the hardwood floor of the hall into a cosy yet spacious open-plan living area. It had modern comforts as well as traditional elegance: the high ceilings and large windows created a sense of airiness, while the furnishings were a tasteful mix of contemporary and antique.

"This is a perfect city retreat," Charlotte mused, looking around.

Angus smiled. "Will it make you change your mind about London?"

"Not at all. What are we looking for?"

"I don't know. Probably nothing, but we need to have a look around, in case he's been living here all the time."

"Yes, because those video doorbells are easy to hack."

They went into the bedroom. One side of the super king-size bed had been slept in, and the bedspread was still turned down. A towel lay crumpled at the bottom of the shower tray in the en-suite bathroom, and the shelf above the sink held a toothbrush and a tube of toothpaste.

Angus looked through the wardrobe, then the drawers. There were a few items in both.

"Nothing looks out of place to me," Charlotte commented. She took out her laptop and typed at it. Then she walked over to the chest of drawers, turned over the Wi-Fi router and typed in the password. "It's so much easier to snoop around someone's network when you have the password," she mused, not looking up.

Angus was on his hands and knees, peering under the bed. He got to his feet. "What can you find out from the router?"

"If Lawrence connected his phone to the Wi-Fi instead of using mobile data, he'll have left me a nice little trail." She sat down on the corner of the bed and typed. Then she frowned. "That's interesting. He used a VPN."

"Virtual Private Network," Angus said.

"Very impressive, Mr Technophobe."

"Your techno-babble is rubbing off on me. Why is that interesting?"

"It means that he wanted to hide what he was up to."

"Oh. Is there no way for you to find out what he did, then?"

"No. That's the problem – or advantage – of the VPN. They're great at hiding what you're doing on the internet."

"I guess if he wanted to go off-grid, that's the ideal way of doing it."

"Yes, but Cressida said he didn't do technology."

"A lot of people know about VPNs, though."

"Do they? Hmm." Charlotte pondered. "Can you check with Cressida?"

"Sure, if you think he's hiding something. So there's definitely no way to get at his online history?"

"No. Lawrence used a VPN the whole time he was here, and his phone is the only one that's connected. The timestamp of the connection matches the time when we know he was here, from the video doorbell."

"I'll look through the rest of the flat." Angus walked through to the lounge and kitchen and searched the cupboards and drawers. Charlotte followed, not wanting to miss anything. "Not much food in, just a few staples. The kitchen equipment's good, though. I suppose you'd expect that."

"Would you eat out a lot if you were a chef?" Charlotte asked. "If I could cook like him, I'd cook for myself all the time."

Angus inspected a collection of knives hanging on a magnetic board. "These are Wüsthof brand. Expensive. And one's missing..."

Angus checked the dishwasher and everywhere else he could think of. "One knife is definitely missing. I'll check with Cressida: maybe it got damaged and they threw it out."

Charlotte shook her head. "So, a very stressed and angry chef has gone missing, possibly with a knife?"

"We don't know he took the knife. That's quite a jump."

"You'd better check with Cressida, then."

Angus took his phone out and dialled. Charlotte continued to look around the kitchen as he spoke to Cressida and then until he ended the call.

Angus sighed. "She can't remember how many knives there were, or if one was missing."

"Helpful," Charlotte said with irony.

Angus looked around. "All right, I think we've exhausted everything here. Let's head home." They locked up, replaced the key in the safe and went outside, where Grigore was waiting in the Bentley.

Charlotte looked at her watch; it was nearly five o'clock. "Hmmm: I hadn't thought about traffic. Let's stay the night and head back in the morning. I'll book rooms."

Angus thought about protesting, but the thought of a four-hour car journey – possibly minimum – wasn't appealing, even if Grigore was driving and he was in the back of a Bentley. "Okay, where?"

"Let me make a phone call." Charlotte tapped at her phone. "Hello, darling, how are you? Yes, I'm fine, thank you. You'll never guess where I am! How did you know?" She laughed, then glanced at Angus. "Do you have a suite free tonight?" Then added, "Two bedrooms."

There was a pause as she waited for a reply. "You do? Fantastic! I'll be there in a jiffy. I can't wait to see you!" She ended the call and smiled at Angus. "That's us sorted: we have a suite at the Dorchester. The manager there is a lovely woman."

"*What?*"

"You know the way, Grigore?"

Grigore nodded and they set off.

Charlotte looked out of the window as they drove. After a few minutes, she turned to Angus. "I thought you'd protest and make us stay in a Premier Inn."

"There's nothing wrong with a Premier Inn. But I can't see you in one."

Charlotte smiled. "I stayed in my fair share of budget hotels back in the day. The Dorchester is a different kettle of fish."

"I won't ask how much this is going to cost."

"I won't tell you, even if you do ask."

When they arrived and got out of the car, Angus mused that a Bentley arriving was not an unusual occurrence at the Dorchester. The uniformed doorman welcomed them warmly. As they went in, a short, grey-haired woman in her sixties appeared out of nowhere. "Charlotte! How wonderful to see you!"

"Maggie!" They hugged.

Maggie Baxter, as her name badge read, was a formidable presence. By the way she and Charlotte held on to each other, they were good friends.

"It's been too long," Maggie scolded Charlotte. "But it's lovely to see you now. The suite's all ready for you."

Eventually, Charlotte introduced Angus, and they were shown to the suite by Maggie herself.

The suite was the height of luxury. The plush furnishings were all warm neutrals, accented with rich textures and elegant patterns. The main room had a high ceiling, with intricate mouldings and a crystal chandelier.

There were two bedrooms, and Charlotte let Angus choose.

He shrugged. "I don't mind which I take, but I don't have a change of clothes. I was expecting to be home tonight."

"Don't worry," Charlotte said. "The butler will get you everything you need."

"The butler?" Angus shook his head. He couldn't help

noticing that Charlotte looked very at home in these opulent surroundings.

She walked to a small table and picked up the old-fashioned phone. "Hi, it's Charlotte Lockwood. Mr Darrow needs a change of clothes for tomorrow. Can you sort it?" There was a long pause. "Lovely, thanks so much." She put the phone down. "Someone will be up shortly with some clothes for you to choose from."

Angus, who had been stood by the window looking out, turned to Charlotte with a confused expression. "How will they know my size? Do they just keep clothes here in case anyone needs them? Do I keep them or give them back?"

"Questions, questions..." Charlotte tutted with a smile. "To answer: they have a variety of sizes, I don't know and no, you get to keep them."

Angus gave a sigh, then turned to the window. "Nice view. Is that Park Lane?"

She joined him. "Yes. Although it's just a road, it's still a good view."

Charlotte went over to her bag, rummaged and pulled out a small gadget the size of a mobile phone. She switched it on, then held it up as though scanning the room. The display had a green LED, which flashed.

Angus sat down on the nearest sofa. "What are you doing?"

"Scanning for bugs," Charlotte replied, as she moved around the room.

"Scanning for bugs?" Angus laughed. "I doubt this place is infested. It looks sparkling clean." Then he grew serious. "Not the insect kind?"

Charlotte turned to him with a smile. "Not the insect kind: the audio or visual kind." She continued to sweep the room.

Angus blinked. "Why exactly do you think there might be bugs here?"

That made her stop. "Because only the rich or famous can afford to stay here, and they often have interesting things to say. Or they could potentially be blackmailed, if someone catches them in the act of doing something illicit. Before we sold the cybersecurity company, I had several clients who'd been blackmailed with footage from secret cameras in hotels. They hired me to track down who had done it and find any copies."

"What exactly had they done?"

"Nothing illegal: just private moments. I'm sure I don't have to go into any more detail."

"I take it you found the culprits."

Charlotte smiled. "Of course."

Angus frowned. "Wait a minute – what about Grigore? Where is he staying tonight? I assume you aren't sending him back to Devon."

"He's here too: he has his own room. I would never send Grigore to a hotel of a lower standard."

Angus shook his head in disbelief. How the other half live, he thought. Then curiosity got the better of him. "What are we going to do tonight?"

"Something to eat?" Charlotte suggested. "Where do you fancy? We could try a French restaurant. Then you can speak French and order for me."

Angus sat back on the sofa, his arm stretched out to the side. "You'd like that, wouldn't you? I saw a Japanese restaurant not far from here on the way. Honestly, I'd prefer that."

"I'll ask the concierge to book us a table."

Charlotte continued to scan the suite. A few minutes later, she came out of the second bedroom. The gadget now switched off. "The suite's clear: we're not being watched.

Not that Maggie would ever let that happen on her watch, but I needed to be sure."

"You've stayed here before, then?"

"I have, but I got to know Maggie through my old company. A case which involved a very well-known head of state from a prominent European country. I signed an NDA, so I can't tell you anything, but if I ever visit that country, I'm sure of a very warm welcome."

There was a tap at the door. The butler came in, wheeling a mobile clothes rack and handed Angus an overnight bag of toiletries. "I have a selection of clothes for Mr Darrow to choose from."

Charlotte clapped her hands. "Excellent." She went over to the rack and started flicking through the clothes. There was a mix of smart and casual, in a variety of sizes. She picked out a polo shirt and held it up. "I like this."

"Thank you, Charlotte, but I'll pick," Angus said.

"Oh, er, sorry." Charlotte fetched her laptop. "I'll be in my room, working," she said, and gave the butler an apologetic look.

Chapter Eleven

"What should we do about confronting Cameron?" Charlotte asked, picking up a piece of red pepper with her chopsticks. "I can't believe he kept quiet about his argument with Lawrence." They were in Sakura Zen, the Japanese restaurant Angus had seen earlier.

"I've changed my mind. I'll call her," Angus said. "Not now, though. Later, when we're back in the hotel."

They were eating their main course of wagyu beef teppanyaki, after polishing off a starter of grilled miso black cod. Charlotte had ordered the same as Angus, not wanting to make a decision over what to eat.

"Do you think the argument pushed Lawrence over the edge?" Charlotte asked.

Angus selected a piece of beef with his chopsticks. "Possibly. Was there anything else that's gone wrong in his life recently?"

"I don't think so. Cressida didn't mention anything, remember."

"Unless he's been keeping something from her," Charlotte replied. He wouldn't be the first or the last man to do that to his wife," she huffed, recalling her ex-husband Idris's affair with her ex-best friend, Michelle.

There was a lull in the conversation. Then Angus spoke. "I can't help wondering if he's killed himself."

Charlotte stared at him. "What?"

"I know. But men of Lawrence's age are the demographic most likely to commit suicide."

"Wouldn't his body have been found by now?"

"Not if he went somewhere remote. I'm not saying that he has, but Lawrence has had mental health issues in the past, and he's just received some bad news. So we should consider it."

"Cressida will probably refuse to entertain the idea if we suggest it."

"Probably. But we should add it to the list of possible scenarios."

Charlotte took a sip of her green tea. "Doesn't Lawrence have a best friend? A male best friend, I mean."

"Not that we know of. There was no one on the list Cressida gave us."

"That's unusual."

"Maybe. Anyway, let's enjoy our meal. Cameron can wait."

* * *

When they got back to the hotel, Angus sat down on the sofa in the lounge area, took out his mobile and dialled Cameron's number. He put it on speaker so Charlotte could hear. After a few rings, Cameron picked up. "Hello?"

"Mr Wright, it's Angus Darrow."

There was a pause. "Yes, hello. What can I do for you?"

"I've learnt that you had an argument with Lawrence a couple of weeks ago, in your office, because you've cancelled Lawrence's TV show."

Another, longer pause. Then Cameron's cool voice said, "Who told you that?"

"Is it true?"

"Yes," he said, eventually. "Yes, it's true."

"Why did you lie to us this afternoon?"

A small laugh. "I didn't lie. I just didn't think it was relevant. You're looking for Lawrence. Our argument was before he disappeared."

Charlotte caught Angus's eye and shook her head in exasperation, frowning.

"It is relevant. He must have been upset by the news."

"Yes, he was, but Lawrence knows how the business works. He knew each series could be the last. He had a good run: four series. That's more than most of these shows manage."

"Is there anything else you've forgotten to mention? Have you seen or heard from Lawrence, for instance?"

"No," he said, at once. "Really, I haven't."

"And do you know where he might be?"

"As I said before, no."

Angus took a deep, resigned breath. "Right. That'll do for now. Goodnight." He ended the call.

Chapter Twelve

On the drive home the next morning, Angus was deep in thought looking out the window.

"What's on your mind?" Charlotte asked.

Angus shrugged. "I know Cressida said that she'd had their second home in Cornwall checked in case Lawrence was there, but I think we should see for ourselves."

"Question everything. You're right." Charlotte looked at her watch. "The property's near Newquay, right?"

"Mawgan Porth," Angus confirmed. "It's close to Newquay Airport."

Charlotte typed the name into her laptop. "If we leave for Newquay soon after we get back, we could be there by five pm."

"We can leave it until tomorrow, if you prefer."

"No, let's go now. Then we've eliminated all the most obvious places."

On the journey, Charlotte looked up the village on her phone. "Listen to this. All sorts of celebrities have bought properties in Mawgan Porth, squeezing the locals out. No change there, then! Apparently, the place is a ghost town in the winter because of all the holiday homes."

"What sort of celebrities?"

"It's been nicknamed Hollywood On Sea: Cate Blanchett, Noel Gallagher, Kate Winslet and Jason Momoa all have houses there."

"Never heard of the last one."

"Jason Momoa?"

Angus shook his head.

"He was in *Game Of Thrones* and he's Aquaman." Charlotte searched on her phone and showed Angus a picture.

"I've never watched *Game Of Thrones* or *Aquaman*. But I recognise him. Didn't know his name."

"I thought you liked going to the cinema?"

"I do, but not Marvel films."

"Anyway, looking at the photos of the beach, I can understand why people would want to move there. It looks amazing." She read from an online article. "Mawgan Porth beach, nestled on the north coast of Cornwall, is a wide expanse of soft, golden sands framed by rugged cliffs and washed by the Atlantic's frothy waves. This serene spot, a haven for surfers and families alike, comes to life with the rhythmic ebb and flow of the tide, revealing rock pools and caves ripe for exploration."

She scrolled down on her phone. "House prices are high: a few million for a three-bed. No wonder the locals are annoyed."

Angus glanced at her with a smile. "Thinking of moving?"

Charlotte wrinkled her nose. "Topsham suits me. Cornwall is too far from Mark and Fiona. And you, of course.

Besides, I never really enjoyed surfing. Never got the hang of it."

After a short break at home, they set off again, this time in Angus's VW Golf because it was less conspicuous. An hour and a half later, they were on the outskirts of the village. The main road into the village branched. They took the side road and within a couple of minutes pulled up in front of the Westwoods' second home: a sleek, minimalist two-storey house with a white façade and expansive glass windows. In front was a well-manicured lawn, in the middle of which sat a For Sale sign.

"Nice," Angus said, getting out of the car and looking up. "And it's for sale."

"Cressida didn't mention it was for sale, did she?" Charlotte took out her phone. "According to the estate agent's website, it's up for two point five million."

"I wonder if Cressida knows?" Angus said, half to himself.

Charlotte turned to him. "You think Lawrence might have put the house up for sale without telling her?"

Angus shrugged. "It's something we need to check. If he's gone missing because of stress, fair enough, but there might be other reasons, like lack of money."

"I didn't even think of that."

Angus laughed. "Straight out of the mouth of a multi-millionaire!"

"Don't be like that. I mean, I didn't think he'd be in financial difficulties. He's got all sorts of projects on the go. He's on the TV all the time, and there are his books too. Why would he be in financial difficulties?"

"I don't know. But we can't rule it out. Maybe he's been living beyond his means."

They took in the view of the sea and the beach below.

70

The beachgoers were colourful specks against the pale sand that stretched out. Surfers, in dark wetsuits, bobbed up and down in the surf.

Angus pressed the door buzzer.

"It has one of those doorbells with a camera." Charlotte bent and looked into it, then stood up.

Angus rang three times, then knocked, but there was no answer. When he checked, the back gate was locked tight.

"If he's in, he doesn't want to be found. Come on, let's talk to the neighbours." He led the way to a house a little farther down the lane. Outside was a woman in her sixties. She wore jeans and a fitted white shirt and had a short, pixie-style haircut.

"Hi, we're looking for Lawrence Westwood," Angus said. "Have you seen him?"

She frowned at him. "Are you debt collectors, like the last lot? Or just fans?" She said "fans" with a note of disdain in her tone.

"Neither," Charlotte said. "We're friends of Lawrence and his wife and we're concerned about him. Have they been here recently?"

She snorted. "No chance. They've barely been here at all."

"How long have you lived here?"

"Forty years. Well, before most of these Londoners bought their houses. It used to be a lovely place to live, with a great community spirit. Now everyone just comes for the weekend or the summer."

Charlotte and Angus shared a look. "It's the same in Devon," Charlotte said. "That's where we're from."

"I just hope that whoever buys the house lives in it full time. I don't think that's too much to ask, do you?"

Angus leaned forward. "So you've not seen anyone at all at the house?"

The woman shook her head. "Except the debt collectors, not for months."

"Can you remember the company name?"

She narrowed her eyes, thinking. "Began with an A, I think. Can't remember anything else. They flashed their ID cards too quickly for me to see them properly when they called asking about him. Doesn't surprise me, though."

"What?"

"Him getting into debt. All over the TV, all the time. Can't get away from the man. I bet he spends, spends, spends."

"Have the debt collectors been back since?"

"No. I expected them to come back one day and break the door down, but they haven't. Maybe they found them at another of their six houses, or whatever it is, and got the debt paid from that," she said, bitterly.

"How often do Cressida and Lawrence come and stay here?" Charlotte asked.

"Once or twice a year, in the summer. The place is an empty shell the rest of the time. Local families could be living there. Or if they rented it out, at least the local area would get some tourist money. But no, they leave it empty. It shouldn't be allowed." The woman's face contorted with anger.

"Have many people come to look around it now that it's for sale?"

The woman shook her head. "No, but that's no surprise. It's overpriced by at least half a million. Not one local can afford that."

"How long has it been on the market?"

The woman thought for a moment. "Two months, at least. The estate agent could tell you, no doubt."

Angus smiled at her. "Thanks for your help." He handed her one of his cards. "If anyone visits the house, anyone at all, could you let me know?"

She narrowed her eyes, then agreed. "I will."

"I agree with her," Charlotte said, as they got in the car. "There should be a ban on holiday homes. That's why I've never bought one."

Angus turned to her. "You really care about that, don't you?"

"I just think that local communities in beautiful parts of the country shouldn't be ruined by rich Londoners snapping up properties, then leaving them empty most of the time."

"Rich Londoners like you?" He smiled.

"I'm not a Londoner."

"So, Lawrence is being dumped from his TV show, and they've had debt collectors sniffing around. Sounds as if Lawrence has been having more than mental health problems."

Charlotte sighed. "Sounds as if his world is crumbling."

Chapter Thirteen

I t was eight o'clock when they entered Oceanique, Lawrence Westwood's restaurant in Exmouth. Every table was occupied, and the evening service was in full flow. The light, warm summer evening meant that the outside tables were all taken too. Young servers wearing aprons and black trousers, with slicked-back hair, swiftly moved around, attending to every customer's needs.

"Does she know we're coming?" Charlotte asked Angus.

"Yes, but she can only spare us a few minutes."

Charlotte followed Angus to the lectern at the front of the restaurant. A sign dangled from it: *Please wait here for service.* A moment later, one of the smart servers approached them. "Do you have a booking?" she asked, with a smug smile.

Charlotte frowned. "No, we have a personal appointment with Cressida."

The girl nodded. "What name is it?"

"Darrow," Charlotte answered, before Angus could speak. He gave her a look of exasperation, to which she replied with a wide-eyed shrug.

The girl disappeared into the kitchen and Charlotte gazed around her. "Maybe we should have eaten before we came. I'm starving."

There were various plates of food on the tables: sour-dough bread on wooden boards with olive oil and balsamic vinegar for dipping, fried calamari, and plates of white fish with a variety of potatoes and green vegetables. Everything looked delicious.

Angus smiled. "We can go to the chippy again if you like. I'll pay." He meant it as a joke, but Charlotte nodded.

It took a few minutes for Cressida to come out to them. She was red-faced and sweating, and wearing chef's whites. "I'm knee-deep in orders, so this can't take long. Come this way."

She led them through the kitchen, where six chefs were hard at work, and into a small staffroom at the back, with a few chairs and a low coffee table. "What's the news? Have you found him? Because we're all working flat out here."

"We've been busy," Angus said, "but so far there's no trace of him."

"You're not trying hard enough. He's an idiot at times, and absolutely useless at being inconspicuous. It drives me crazy, especially when we're trying to have quiet family time or fly under the radar."

"We've just came back from visiting your Cornwall house."

She stared at Angus. "Why the heck did you go to Cornwall? I told you he wasn't there."

"We needed to make sure."

"You didn't, because I told you about that place. Maureen, from the house up the road, is my eyes and ears there. Nothing gets past her. She might be a curtain twitcher, but she has her uses."

"Did she tell you that the house is up for sale?" Angus countered.

Cressida laughed until she saw Angus wasn't joking. Then she frowned.

"That stupid bastard never liked the house, but it's my sanctuary. Not that I can get there much! If I could, I'd quit all this and move there in an instant. Which estate agent?"

"I have the details in the car. I'll email them to you."

"He's not getting rid of the house that easily. He'll sell it over my dead body!" She put her head in her hands. "What are you playing at, Laurie?" she muttered. Then she looked up at Angus. "You need to find him, pronto. Whatever's going on, this is different to the other times."

"Because he's put the house up for sale?"

"He must have just done it, because Maureen would have seen the sign and told me."

"Unless he asked Maureen to keep quiet about it."

"What? No chance. Lawrence has barely even spoken to Maureen. She's my contact, not his: he leaves all that stuff to me. I'll contact the estate agent in the morning and tell them to take it off the market. Have you got any other nasty surprises for me?"

Angus pushed his glasses up his nose. "According to a neighbour, debt collectors visited the house recently."

"Debt collectors?" Cressida cried. "For goodness sake, what is going on?" Her tone was low and bitter.

"Do you think that could be related to why he's disappeared?"

"I don't know. Maybe."

"It might be prudent to check your bank accounts," Angus said, feeling sorry for Cressida.

Cressida looked up. "I logged into the current account two days ago, when you visited for the first time, so that I could pay you. Everything looked normal then. But we have a number of savings accounts, too, so I'll check those. Is there anything else?" She looked tired, defeated.

"Not yet. Yesterday we visited Liz in Wales, and there was no sign of him there. She hasn't heard from him for months. We've also checked out the London flat, which was clean, and had spoken to Cameron Wright. The main thing we learnt there was that Lawrence is being dropped from his TV show – his replacement will be announced soon – and they'd argued a few weeks ago, about that." He watched Cressida's face as he spoke.

Cressida showed no surprise. "I knew about the TV show. I'm in talks with another channel who are interested in using Lawrence. They want him to be in a new show where top chefs visit restaurants in disguise and rate them. It's called *Secret Service Chefs*."

A server came into the room: she looked stressed. "Boss, we've got an issue with one of the customers. Can you come and sort it out?"

Cressida rolled her eyes and stood up. "Sorry, I have to go. Keep looking." She strode out, muttering.

Angus and Charlotte stood up to go, but instead of leaving, the server came into the room and closed the door. "Are you the detectives looking for Laurie?"

"That's right," Angus said.

The server glanced at the door.

"Do you know something?" Charlotte asked, in a soft tone.

She shrugged.

"If there's something we should know, please tell us. It doesn't matter how insignificant you think it is: it could be useful," Charlotte urged.

"There was a bloke used to work here. Robbie Harper. He was stalking Lawrence."

Angus frowned. "Stalking? How?"

"He kept turning up here at night, when we'd all finished and Lawrence was closing up. Had a go at Lawrence when he was about to drive home. Hung around randomly outside the restaurant when Lawrence would see him."

"Does Cressida know?"

She shook her head. "He didn't want to tell her because Robbie's his dealer. Keeps him in grass."

Angus raised his eyebrows. "Lawrence smokes weed?"

"Only when Cressida's not around: she'd smell it a mile off. Robbie started nicking stuff. Not small stuff that no one would miss; he was going for steaks and lobster. Lawrence found out and sacked him."

"How did he find out?"

"He suspected, and caught him red-handed one night. He didn't tell Cressida, though: he just said that Robbie had left. Robbie's been hassling Lawrence ever since."

"When did this all kick off?"

"Couple of months ago."

"Where does Robbie live?" Angus took out his notebook and pen to write it down.

"Exmouth somewhere. He never said where exactly, but I'm pretty sure he's local."

"Did he ever threaten Lawrence, do you know?"

"Robbie likes to talk himself up, but he's small time. If you met him, you'd see what I mean. I don't think he'd try anything on, but I guess you never know. And by the way, none of this came from me."

"We understand that you're telling us this in confidence." Angus replied.

The door opened and Cressida put her head round it. "Lydia, I need you out front."

"Sorry, boss. Just getting a drink." Lydia opened a locker and pulled out a metal bottle.

"You can get water out the front any time," Cressida huffed, then disappeared back to the restaurant.

Chapter Fourteen

They walked back along the seafront. "Lawrence has a lot of secrets from Cressida," Charlotte said, thoughtfully. "Just like Idris had from me."

Angus glanced at her. "It's not normal to be that secretive with your spouse, you know."

"I don't doubt you were an open book to Rhona when you were married, but how can you be sure that she didn't keep secrets from you? She's a politician after all."

Angus sighed. "Still cynical about relationships, then?"

"No! But since we've been working together, we've uncovered a shedload of deceit and lies. It feels as if everyone has something to hide."

"Which means that we behave differently in our relationships."

"We'd never behave that way, would we?" Charlotte said. But her brief fling with David was on her mind, along with the fact that she'd kept her multimillionaire status from him. That wasn't deceit, was it? Her financial status had no bearing on their attraction to each other. She'd ended the relationship because she hadn't wanted anything to get in the way of the possibility that she and Angus might get together. Nothing had happened on that front, though, even though she'd told Angus several times that she'd finished with David. Now she just had to live in hope that things would change. She wasn't sure, but sometimes it felt as if Angus had feelings for her which ran deeper than friendship. She wondered if Angus not making a move was some sort of karma because she wasn't honest about David.

Charlotte shook herself. It will all work out, she told herself. Misty, her therapist, thought that she should tell Angus how she felt. Helena had said that too. She thought that if Angus didn't feel the same way, he wouldn't let it affect their work, or their working relationship. Charlotte wasn't so sure. She imagined what it would be like working with Angus after he'd rejected her for a second time. It would be humiliating. Awkward. And she realised that she would probably have to finish working with him.

As they passed the lifeboat building, Charlotte and Angus noticed that the new swimming lockers outside had been cordoned off with police tape. They'd been smashed. The damage looked as if it had been done by a claw hammer.

"I saw on social media that those lockers have only been here a few weeks," Angus said. "The locals are livid."

"I'm not surprised," Charlotte replied. "Those lockers were supposed to help raise money for the life boats. Who's desperate enough to steal from swimming lockers?"

They stopped in front of them. "Drug addicts, probably," Angus said. "They'll steal anything to get their next fix. Most petty theft is due to drugs."

"That's why I never took any drugs: I knew I'd get addicted straight away if I did. I never smoked either. I tried it once and almost threw up."

"Looks like they opened every locker," Angus said. "There's another set of lockers at the other end of the quay. If I were the police, I'd point a camera at them."

Charlotte raised her eyebrows.

Angus studied her. "You're going to put a camera on them, aren't you?"

"Totally."

"Honestly, I don't think it's worth it. Like I said, it'll be a petty thief. If you catch them, all they'll get is a slap on the wrist from the magistrate, and they'll be back making mischief as soon as they can."

"Cynical," Charlotte said.

"Just the truth."

"Well, I'm going to put a camera on it and see what – or who – turns up."

"That's up to you."

She scanned the seafront. "Where would you put the camera? There isn't anywhere, really, just a hotel opposite."

"If I was going to set something up," Angus said, thoughtfully, "I'd probably put a burner phone in a locker, wait for it to be stolen, then track it."

"That's a brilliant idea!" Charlotte clapped her hands together and jumped up and down. "I'll get one from home and bring it over. Then we just have to wait."

Angus raised his eyebrows. "We?"

Charlotte sighed.

* * *

Charlotte chose a recent-model iPhone as the bait for the locker thief. She charged it up and loaded hidden software on to it, then Grigore drove her the fifteen minutes it took from Topsham to Exmouth. Charlotte picked a locker, placed the phone inside with a small jacket, put her pound coin in, and locked it, taking the key. Then she got back in the car. "Do you think they'll rob the lockers tonight?"

Grigore shrugged. "Maybe."

"Do you think this is silly?" Charlotte asked. "Angus thought so."

"I no judge. You do what you like vether I approve or no."

"That's true, but I do value your opinion."

"I zink you waste your time. But it your time to waste," Grigore said, looking at her through the rear-view mirror.

Charlotte sighed. "You may be right. But petty theft like this can ruin a town if it's allowed to continue."

"Better to get drug gang and stop ze drugs. That stops stealing. They root cause."

"I'm sure my brother is on the case, along with the other police in the area. I bet they know who all the people are. Anyway, I bet there's more than one drugs gang operating in most towns."

"That probable."

"Drive me home, please, Grigore. Now we just have to wait and see if the phone gets stolen. The phone will alert me if it's moved from its current location."

That night, Charlotte watched her phone for an alert, and she even checked the phone's location a few times, but it remained undisturbed in the locker.

Chapter Fifteen

The next day, Angus and Charlotte returned to Exmouth to look into Robbie Harper. Charlotte had searched the internet and found out that Robbie's house was in The Colonies, the nickname for an area of Exmouth near the train station. It had rows of Victorian terraced houses, similar to those all over the country.

When they drove up to Robbie's house there was no room to park outside. Angus drove past, then pulled up farther down the road on double yellow lines.

Charlotte opened her laptop and tried to work out which Wi-Fi might be his. After a few minutes, she sighed. "There are too many. I can't work out which is Robbie's, assuming he has Wi-Fi! I need to walk past the house to get a clearer picture."

It was still light, and a few people were walking along the street. "How can I do this without looking suspicious and ending up on a Facebook page as a suspicious character?" Charlotte wondered aloud.

"Just pretend you're on FaceTime with a friend," Angus said. "Lots of people do that. I find it very irritating."

"I know!" Charlotte exclaimed. "If I could ban anything, it would be people who did that. All right, I'll give it a go."

She got out of the car and walked towards Robbie's house. When she got near, she took out her phone and held it in front of her. "How are you, hon? I heard about you and Freddie. Was it a bad break-up? I've been through it myself; you should have called me." She reached Robbie's house and stopped. "I know!" she said, into the phone. "We have to meet for coffee soon, yeah?" Charlotte tapped on the screen, letting her program triangulate the nearest Wi-Fis. It took ten seconds. "Great, let's meet in that café on the seafront!" she said, as she walked back towards Angus's VW Golf.

As soon as she'd shut the car door, Charlotte opened her laptop again. "That was easy. I won't win any Oscars for acting, but at least I didn't look as if I was lurking for no reason. I don't think anyone noticed me, anyway. I should get one of those hi-vis work coats. That works: a clipboard and a luminous coat. No one questions it. I bet I'll forget, though."

Angus waited patiently for her to finish. "Does he have Wi-Fi?" he asked.

"I think so. There were two, and I think these are maisonettes, so I'll have to crack both and see what I can find."

An hour later, Charlotte had cracked both Wi-Fis, put her sniffing software on to the networks and discovered that neither Wi-Fi was Robbie's.

"We need another way to find out about him."

"Stakeout?"

"Possibly." Angus peered through the car window. "But this is a densely populated area: we'll be spotted quickly."

"I have an idea."

Angus's eyes narrowed. "Is it legal?"

Charlotte considered. "I would have to say maybe. But that doesn't matter, because what I have in mind is untraceable."

"Untraceable? Then it's a no from me."

"You haven't even heard my idea!"

"There are plenty of ways to find out what we need to without some illegal hacking technique. Like knocking on his door and asking him if we can come in."

"All right, you try that and see what happens. And if Robbie says no, I'll deploy my plan."

Angus eyed Charlotte. "You'll do it even if I say no, won't you?" He undid his seatbelt. "I'll try and talk to him."

Charlotte gave a shrug with one shoulder and watched as he got out.

Angus walked to Robbie's house under Charlotte's close scrutiny. When he neared the door, she got out of the car and watched him knock. Angus looked down the street and Charlotte ducked.

She heard him knock again. There was no response. As he turned, Charlotte got back in the car, closing the door quietly. "He wasn't in, then?" she asked, when Angus returned.

"No. We can come back later and try again. In the meantime, continue your internet searches and see what you can find out about Robbie Harper."

Chapter Sixteen

Angus dropped Charlotte home before heading back to Exeter. As soon as his car had left, Charlotte began to contemplate when would be a good time to return and try her scheme. She decided on early afternoon and considered wearing a disguise. In the end, she decided against it.

This time, Robbie was in.

"Hi, are you Robbie Harper?" she asked when he opened the door.

"Yeah." Robbie was unshaven, with tousled brown hair and a sturdy build. He was dressed casually in tracksuit bottoms and a well-worn blue T-shirt. He looked older than she expected.

"I'm from a local market research company. We're just doing a survey about internet coverage. In some areas of Devon, internet coverage is an absolute nightmare, and we want to know your views. Do you have a minute to help me?"

Robbie shrugged. "I don't use the internet, really. Sorry, love."

Charlotte gave a low titter. "There's a ten-pound M&S Food voucher if you can help. You can splash out at the store down the road."

"All right, then."

Charlotte looked at her tablet computer. "Do you use a mobile phone?"

"Well, yeah, I use the internet on that, but it costs a fortune for data. So I don't use it much."

"Oh, that's interesting." Charlotte tapped on her tablet again. "Can I make a note of your comments?"

"Er, yeah, I suppose so."

"Who is your current broadband provider?"

"Ain't got one. Just use my phone."

"Interesting... Thank you. So when you do use the internet, what sort of things do you do? Web browsing? Games? Any apps?"

Robbie leant against the doorframe. "WhatsApp mainly. Sometimes I order food on Deliveroo, but not much else."

"No streaming or Netflix or anything like that?"

"No, love. Sorry. Like I said, the data is expensive."

"Thank you so much. Can I just ask you a few questions to finish off the survey? First, your age."

"Twenty-seven."

"Ethnic origin: White British. Is that correct?"

"Yeah."

"And are you married, in a relationship, single...?"

"Single."

"And what is your job?"

"I'm a chef at the budget hotel on the seafront." Robbie's eyebrows drew together. "Don't see why you need to know that."

Charlotte tapped at her iPad. "It's just to get an idea of

who is answering the questions so we can cover people of different backgrounds and jobs."

Robbie gave a small nod.

"So that goes in food and hospitality. Perfect. Thank you so much! Now, if you can give me your phone number, I'll send you the link for a ten-pound voucher which you can spend at the Marks and Spencer Food Hall in the town."

Robbie gave her the number, Charlotte tapped it into the tablet, and she heard a buzz from Robbie's pocket. "There you go. Just click the link in the message and it will take you to a QR code which you scan in store."

Robbie fished out his smartphone. It had a large crack on the screen. He clicked, and the QR code appeared. "Cheers, love."

"No. Thank you." Charlotte smiled. "Bye."

Grigore pulled away from his parking spot round the corner. She got in and then sat back. "So easy. People are so stupid."

"What you do?" Grigore asked.

"I just got him to install a hidden virus on his phone. Now I can track everything he does, and it won't ever show up. I can listen in to every conversation, read every text. I can even switch on his phone camera remotely."

Grigore looked at her in the rear-view mirror. "I hope I never cross you."

Charlotte smiled. "We'll be friends for ever, Grigore. Remember the *Vortex*."

He nodded remembering the nightclub, and Charlotte smiled.

"Right, now to switch on the tracker and watch it harvest all the data from his phone." She beamed as she pressed the button.

Chapter Seventeen

It was Saturday lunchtime. Charlotte and Angus were in Sidmouth to meet Angus's parents at the folk festival. After various messages back and forth, they found Gordon and Eileen in Blackmore Gardens, the heart of the event. They were sitting on one of many wooden picnic benches. A huge marquee had been set up, and inside a dance workshop was in full flow. A few people were sitting on picnic blankets on the lawn, eating street food from the stalls. There was a general ambience of a family festival with people milling around and having a good time.

Gordon and Eileen didn't see them approach, as they were talking to someone. As they drew nearer, Charlotte suppressed a groan.

Rhona. Angus's ex-wife.

"Angus! Charlotte!" Gordon shouted, and waved when he caught sight of them.

Rhona turned, and her smile disappeared the moment she set eyes on Charlotte. That gave Charlotte a moment of pleasure.

"Come and sit next to me," Eileen said to Angus.

Angus seated himself beside his mother and nodded to Rhona.

"You came!" said Gordon as Charlotte took the only seat left, next to Rhona.

"Of course! How could I miss getting to know the father of my favourite man in all the world?" Charlotte glanced at Rhona, whose left eye twitched. Angus was already in deep conversation with his mother and hadn't heard the exchange.

"How has the festival been so far, Gordon?" Charlotte asked, ignoring Rhona.

"Grand, grand. I was just telling Rhona here that we've been busy. So many workshops to choose from and ceilidhs every night."

Charlotte looked at Gordon's almost empty pint glass. "Can I get you a drink?"

Gordon looked rather embarrassed. "Oh, I've never let a woman buy me a drink yet."

"There's a first time for everything," Charlotte said, standing up. She collected Gordon's glass, then put her hand on Angus's shoulder to get his attention, making sure Rhona could see. "Drink?"

Angus looked up and smiled. "Just a Coke, thanks."

"Eileen?"

"Thank you very much. Same again for me: gin and tonic."

Charlotte let her hand rest on Angus's shoulder for a moment. "Rhona?"

Rhona looked up. "Not for me, thanks."

When Charlotte returned with the drinks, Rhona seemed much more cheerful. "Oh look, there's Izzy Carter!" she gushed. "I love her so much!" She leaned towards

Eileen. "Do you think she'd mind if I asked for her autograph?"

Charlotte followed Rhona's gaze and saw a short woman dressed in boho clothes, surrounded by a small entourage. The crowd had also recognised her and were vying for her attention as she mingled.

"Never heard of her," Charlotte commented and sipped her Coke.

Rhona tutted. "She's folk royalty."

"I'll take your word for it."

"She's headlining tomorrow night at The Ham marquee," Rhona stated, looking superior.

"Sadly, I'll be washing my hair."

Rhona scowled, then turned to Gordon. "Do you remember the time Grace did the piano accordion workshop? What year was that?"

Gordon laughed. "Oh aye, I remember. That was a memorable festival. You could barely see the wee lass: the accordion was that big and she was so small."

Rhona turned to her ex-husband. "Hey, Angus, do you remember that year?"

Angus looked over at the sound of his name. His gaze fell on Charlotte for a moment, and then he looked at Rhona. "Sorry, which year?"

Rhona gave an exasperated sigh. "The one where Grace did the accordion workshop, Angus."

"I thought she did that a few years in a row."

"No, she definitely didn't."

The atmosphere in the gardens and the town was relaxed yet vibrant. Even though Charlotte wasn't a fan of folk music, the festival was a fun place to be. It was almost perfect. Almost, because it would have been much better without Rhona.

Rhona made a point of reminiscing at length about previous years' festivals, and Charlotte suspected she was doing it to exclude her from the conversation. She excused herself in the middle of a particularly rambling anecdote to visit the stalls at the far side of the gardens. These sold musical instruments, jewellery and the kind of tie-dyed and patchwork clothes you might see folk royalty wearing.

Charlotte was just admiring the paintings of a local artist when Angus came over. "You okay?"

She smiled at him. Her previous disgruntled thoughts vanished. "I'm fine. I just couldn't take any more of Rhona. How did you put up with her for so long?"

Angus shook his head, smiling back at her. "Ever honest. Well, at least you walked away from the situation."

"What is she doing here, anyway? Has she come just to annoy me? And where's her boyfriend?"

"I have no idea about her partner, and she's here because, despite being divorced from me, she still gets on with my mum and dad."

"That's so strange. I don't contact Idris's parents: they're an odd pair, anyway. And my mum and dad were ready to stab Idris in the heart for what he did to me."

"You've never talked about your parents before."

"Haven't I?" Charlotte shrugged and carried on to the next stall, which sold secondhand jewellery. "I get on with my parents, but they're permanently on a cruise."

"Paid for by you?"

Charlotte picked up a necklace and looked at it.

"That's just two pounds today," the stallholder said quickly.

Charlotte nodded. "Yes, paid for by me. I gave them the money, but I didn't expect them to disappear all the time."

"Is that why you don't talk about them?"

Charlotte took out her purse and handed over a two-pound coin. "Only because I never see them."

"So your best friend and husband have an affair, and your parents sail off into the sunset. No wonder you moved to be near your brother. I assume you spoke to Misty about all of it?"

Charlotte walked to the next stall. "Of course I have. But I don't resent my parents going. I can fly to wherever they are whenever I want." As long as we meet off the cruise ship."

"But you're not happy."

Charlotte half shrugged. "I'm happy that they're happy, but I'd like to see them more. And when it all went pear-shaped with Idris, they'd already left, so they couldn't give me a great deal of support. That's why Mark and Fiona mean so much to me."

They stopped walking and faced each other. Angus put his hand on Charlotte's arm. "I understand. When my parents moved back to Scotland, I wasn't happy about it either. But I get to see them a few times a year, so it's not that different really. They haven't disappeared halfway round the world, though."

Charlotte looked back to the picnic table, where Rhona and Gordon were laughing about something. Charlotte's eyes narrowed, then she looked back at Angus. "Your parents are lovely. But you turned out well, so that's not a surprise."

Angus replied, amused, "Another compliment. I'll try not to let it go to my head."

The spell was broken by an alarm on Charlotte's phone. She fished it out and checked the display, and her expression changed. "Oooh. The locker phone in Exmouth is on the move. Someone's broken into the locker and pinched it. I'd nearly forgotten about it."

Angus leaned in and peered at the phone.

"I'll switch the camera on remotely," Charlotte said. "Maybe I can see who has it." She clicked a few buttons, and the screen changed to show video. "The screen's black: they must have put it in a bag." She held her phone to her ear, then shook her head. "Can't hear anything. Guess I'll need to track it."

"I'll come too."

"No, you stay with your parents."

"And leave you to a showdown with God knows who? I don't think so."

"I won't confront them; I'll just stake them out."

"Or hack their Wi-Fi."

"We'll wait for it to stop moving before we leave. That way, you can spend more time with your parents." Charlotte hoped Rhona would take herself off somewhere. If not, she'd work on some snippy comments.

"All right," Angus said. "But I'm coming with you when you go after that phone."

Chapter Eighteen

The phone was on the move for nearly an hour. It went to Exmouth harbour, then into a pizza place before coming to what seemed to be a permanent halt in a house in the town centre.

Charlotte looked up the address. "It says it's owned by a building company."

"It's probably being renovated."

"I'll look on Google Maps." She put in the address and examined the photos. "This mightn't be any help: the photos were taken eight years ago. That's way too old to be any use."

"We need to check the place out," Angus said.

Charlotte stood up. "All right, let's go."

It took them nearly half an hour to get to Exmouth. Angus parked a few doors down, on the opposite side of the road. "It looks different to Google Maps," he said.

The house in question was a tall, brick-built end terrace with boarded-up windows.

"There may be squatters in there. Which means we need to be very careful when we go in."

Charlotte raised her eyebrows. "I thought we weren't going in."

Angus glanced at Charlotte. "We'll keep watch for a while to see if anyone comes in or out. If I think it's safe, we'll go in."

An hour later, nothing had happened. Charlotte huffed. "Maybe I should have just left it. Petty theft's bad, but it isn't worth this amount of our time. Shouldn't we be looking for Lawrence? Or at least spending some more time with your parents?"

They went up to the front door and Angus tried it. It was open, so they crept in.

Inside was a mess. The walls were dirty and there was no carpet, just bare floorboards. The stairs were uncarpeted, too, and a number of rooms led off the hall, including what looked like a very dirty kitchen straight ahead.

Charlotte took out her phone to locate the burner phone. "It's upstairs," she whispered.

Angus went up first. The first floor had three rooms. Charlotte shook her head, then pointed upstairs. The top floor had two rooms. Charlotte moved her head towards the door on the left, which was ajar. Angus knocked, then pushed the door.

Inside was a teenage girl sitting on a bed. Her greasy brown hair was in a ponytail and she wore a T-shirt and sweatpants. "Who are you?" she said, scowling at them.

"No, who are you?" Charlotte said.

"None of your business."

"We're private investigators and you have my mobile phone," Charlotte said, before Angus could open his mouth.

The girl stood up and glanced at the door. Angus and Charlotte moved in front of it.

"I ain't got nothing," she said, eyeing them warily.

Charlotte tapped her phone and another phone rang.

"That's my phone. You stole it from the locker on the seafront."

The ringing was coming from a plastic bag on the table in the corner. Angus went towards it and the girl bolted for the door. Charlotte grabbed her as she was heading through it. Angus helped her pull the girl back into the room. Charlotte shut the door firmly.

The girl shook herself free, then sat back on the bed.

"What's your name?" Angus asked.

She looked at the floor. "Ain't telling you."

Charlotte gasped. "You're the missing girl I saw on social media a few days ago!"

"No, I'm not," she said, looking away.

"You are," Charlotte said. "I saw your photo on Facebook."

"I'm eighteen, I can do what I like."

"Like stealing?"

Angus crouched down to look into her face. "Are you on drugs?"

"No. I don't do that stuff: it messes you up. I don't want to get messed up."

Charlotte and Angus looked at each other, neither of them convinced.

Angus looked around the bare room. "So you're not stealing for drugs?"

"No."

"Why are you stealing, then?"

She shrugged. "Food, innit."

"Have you thought about getting a job?" Charlotte asked in a more patronising tone than she intended.

The girl didn't reply.

"It's easier to steal things, I suppose," Angus said. "In the short term."

Charlotte softened her voice. "You can't do this for ever, you know. We've caught you, and you'll get caught again."

"I don't normally steal," she said, in a sad tone.

"Ha, so you admit it!" She turned to Angus. "Is it normal for kids like this to steal for things other than drugs?"

"Not usually. Sometimes gangs steal designer goods to sell on, but usually it's all drug related."

"Put your hood down!" Charlotte snapped. "And look at me when I'm talking to you."

The girl looked up at her, sighed, then put down her hood.

Charlotte moved closer and examined her. "Hmm. You don't look like you're on drugs. You could do with a good wash, though."

"Shut up." The girl looked away.

"Her name is Kaylee Smith, and she's from Newton Abbott," Angus read from his phone screen.

Charlotte looked over, impressed. "Check you out, using the internet!"

Angus ignored that. "She's eighteen, and she's been missing for a few weeks."

Charlotte sat on the bed beside Kaylee. "Why did you run away?"

Kaylee shrugged.

"There must be a reason. Problems at home?"

Kaylee fidgeted with her hands. "My mum got a new bloke," she said, eventually.

Angus and Charlotte stayed silent.

"He's nasty to me. Wants me out the house."

"Why's that?"

"He wants Mum all to himself. He's controlling."

"Tell you what," Charlotte said. "I've got a friend who helps girls like you sort their lives out. If you come with us now, I'll take you to her, and I'll make all the evidence that you've been stealing go away. You can stay there as long as you need—"

"I'm not going with you!" Kaylee shouted. "Why should I trust you?"

"What have you got to lose? You're living in a squat and stealing to feed yourself."

"You ain't blackmailing me into going with you."

"Then I'll have to report you to the police."

The girl shrugged. "Don't care."

"The refuge is all women."

"I don't believe you! You're going to pimp me out!" Kaylee jumped to her feet. "I ain't being no sex worker!"

Charlotte recoiled. "*What?* No! I would never do that! And what you're talking about isn't sex work. It's prostitution, plain and simple. Sex work makes it sound as if women choose to do it."

"Charlotte..." Angus put a hand on Charlotte's arm. "She doesn't trust us, and we can't make her come with us. That's kidnapping."

The girl looked at Angus, a glimmer of hope in her eyes.

Charlotte folded her arms. "Fine," she snapped. Then she turned to Kaylee. "You don't know a good offer when you see one. But I'll give you my number. If you change your mind, call me: day or night. I can help you start a new life. One where you don't have to nick things to stay alive."

Charlotte picked up the stolen phone and typed in her number. Then she reached into her bag, got her purse, pulled out a small wad of notes and handed them to the girl. "Take this and stay out of trouble."

Kaylee looked at the money, then at Charlotte.

"No strings," Charlotte stated.

Kaylee took the money.

Angus opened the door and walked out, and Charlotte followed.

Outside the building, Angus halted. "You can't help someone who doesn't want to be helped, Charlotte. If she changes her mind, she'll contact you."

Charlotte sighed. "I know. It's so frustrating, though. I could help her – really help her."

"Considering her age, she seems to have her head screwed on." Angus smiled. "When the cash runs out, maybe she'll give you a chance."

Chapter Nineteen

The next morning, Angus arrived at Charlotte's house. When Charlotte opened the front door, she was still in her pyjamas. Angus tried not to make it obvious he was giving her the once-over.

"Late night?"

Charlotte yawned. "Just work."

He followed her in.

"How did it go at the folk festival last night?" Charlotte asked as they reached the kitchen. Angus had returned to Sidmouth and his parents after they'd left Kaylee.

"It was okay: we went to a small gig in one of the pubs. Some folk duet I'd never heard of. They were good, though."

"I'd like to see your parents again. They're nice."

"They like you too."

Charlotte's eyes widened, then she beamed. "They said that?"

Angus smiled. "It would be hard not to like you."

Charlotte snorted. "Tell that to my ex-husband and his mistress."

Angus winced. "I'm hoping I never have to meet him again." Angus took out his notebook. "Anyway, to business. What did you discover the other night when you checked out Robbie Harper?"

Charlotte gaped at him. "What makes you think I checked him out?"

Angus chuckled. "Grigore kept me up to date. I knew you'd go, but I wanted to make sure you didn't do anything stupid."

"The turncoat!" Then she sighed. "Grigore looks after me."

"He does. He said something about a virus on Robbie's phone?"

Charlotte stood up, picked up a few pages from the printer tray and handed them to Angus. "There's no evidence that Robbie's been stalking Lawrence over the last few weeks. However, there's also no sign of Lawrence in Robbie's house. But he has hung around Oceanique a couple of times a few weeks ago."

Angus glanced at the printout. "What's this?"

"Data from Robbie's mobile."

Angus closed his eyes. "You have access to his phone?"

"Of course. I put a virus on it, as you know from Grigore. It's untraceable, and it gives me total access."

Angus reached for the chair behind him and sat down, then put his hand over his face. "If the police find out what you've done, you'll be in prison for years. Putting yourself at risk like this is stupid." It didn't matter how safe she thought she was, the thought of her locked up for years gave him a bad feeling in the pit of his stomach.

Charlotte shrugged. "Stupid? I'm not stupid. They won't know it's me. The software is untraceable: it deletes itself. It's an exact copy of the Pegasus software, which lots of governments use but claim they don't. They think they're the only ones with the ability to create this type of software, but they're not."

"Did you write it?"

"No. A friend who owes me lots of favours did, and it's *very* useful."

"When you say you have access to Robbie's phone, do you mean everything?"

Charlotte nodded.

"Like, *everything* everything?"

"Yup. His data, call logs, GPS, camera and audio. I switched the phone's camera and audio on, and he was on his own. That's how I know Lawrence isn't in his house. He hasn't kidnapped Lawrence, or anything like that. He is a small-time drug dealer, though. He deals in low-level stuff – weed, MDMA – and legal highs. From some of his text messages, I'd say that Lawrence owes him money. That's why Robbie's been stalking him, to get what he's owed. It's nothing to do with being sacked for stealing."

Angus sighed. "I think I preferred it when you hacked people's Wi-Fis. How is this technology even possible?"

Charlotte's eyes lit up. "Exploits."

"What do noble deeds have to do with computers?"

"Not that type of exploit. Technological exploits. There are lots of them, in all operating systems. They all have flaws, and if you know what they are, you can exploit them. And not just mobile phones: computers too. If you know how to hack the memory and the CPU, it's easy – you just need a way in. Most of the time, you don't even need the person to click anything. It can be done remotely, but my program has to be clicked. That's the only difference between my version and Pegasus. It's untraceable, and it deletes itself if anyone tries to look for it."

Angus's eyes had glazed over. "I didn't need a techie explanation."

Charlotte shrugged. "Sorry. But you did ask."

Angus's eyes narrowed. "You haven't put this on my phone, have you?"

Charlotte stared at him. "No! How could you even think of such a thing? I'd never do that. I only use this when it's absolutely necessary."

Angus studied her without speaking.

"You're doing that police thing, aren't you? Trying to work out if I'm telling the truth."

"Of course I am."

She tilted her head. "Well, am I lying?"

Angus sighed. "No. But please, for the sake of our work and friendship, never put that thing on my phone. Do you understand? That would be a step too far."

Charlotte gave a tight smile. "I won't."

Angus turned to the conspiracy board. "So Robbie hasn't kidnapped Lawrence. Lawrence is a drug user. We need to look into the possibility that he's taken an overdose or is trouble with a drug gang."

Charlotte grimaced at the thought of Lawrence's rotting body lying somewhere deserted. "Where would he have gone to take drugs? Would he have done that at home, or at work? What would be his drug of choice?"

"Cocaine is still the drug of choice for people like him," Angus said. "But Lydia said he smoked weed earlier. Maybe he dabbled with both."

"So he's probably been taking it at work, then, if that's where he spent most of his time and where he met up with Robbie."

Angus tapped his pen against his lips, pondering. "I'm not sure, but yes, we need to find out. It's low level, and if he can't pay his dealer, presumably he's having to do without. But I like to cover everything. I'll call Cressida and see whether she knows about his drug taking."

Angus picked up his phone and opened the door that led to the garden. A few minutes later, he reappeared. "Cressida knew about the drugs. She said it was weed mainly. She said Lawrence thought she didn't know, but as it was just weed, she didn't bother him about it."

"Why didn't she tell us?"

"She didn't think it was relevant."

Charlotte rolled her eyes.

"To be fair, she did say that Lawrence had been clean for a while, but he relapsed a couple of months ago."

"Did she know that Robbie was his dealer?"

"I didn't mention Robbie, but she didn't know who his dealer was. My gut feeling is that this is nothing to do with him going missing. If Lawrence has been taking coke for a while, like Lydia said, he was probably using it to give himself a buzz. Maybe he needed some kind of euphoria if his life was unhappy. I can't see him getting into debt for it, though. He could easily pay for it."

"Maybe he did a bit of dealing himself?" Charlotte said.

Angus shook his head. "I don't think so. It would be pretty risky for someone in his position."

Charlotte studied her computer screen. "Looking at the data on Robbie's phone, he hasn't been near the restaurant or the Westwoods' home in weeks. It also looks as if he's got a new job. He told me he worked at the budget hotel on the seafront."

"Maybe we should just ask him if he's been stalking Lawrence."

"He'll recognise me," Charlotte said.

"Then I'll go alone."

Chapter Twenty

Instead of going to Robbie's house, Angus decided to see him at work. The hotel he was employed at had been built a few years before. It offered all-you-can-eat English breakfasts for a very reasonable price for both residents and non-residents.

Angus had stayed in his fair share of budget hotels over the years and knew the drill. He went inside and was greeted by a server, who took his payment, then told him to choose a table and help himself.

Angus raided the breakfast buffet: bacon, sausages, beans, black pudding, mushrooms, eggs, tomatoes, hash browns and a cup of tea.

"Is Robbie working today?" he asked the server, when he'd finished eating.

"Yeah, he is. You a friend?"

Angus had prepared an answer that wasn't exactly a lie. He gave the server a friendly smile. "No, but we have mutual acquaintances. Could you get him? I'd like a word."

The woman nodded and went into the kitchen.

Robbie came out dressed in chef's whites, and the server pointed Angus out.

Angus stood up as Robbie approached the table. "Hi, Robbie, have a seat."

Robbie eyed Angus's empty plate suspiciously. "Everything all right?"

"Oh yes." Angus indicated a chair and Robbie sat down. Angus resumed his seat. "I just wanted a quick word."

Robbie looked at him cautiously, then glanced around him as though he were doing something he shouldn't.

"Great breakfast," Angus said. "You've not been here long?"

"Ta, and no. Who are you?"

Angus leaned forward and lowered his voice. "I'll cut to the chase. I work for Cressida Westwood."

Robbie scowled. "That bitch."

"I know things went pear-shaped when you worked with Lawrence. Have you seen him lately?"

"Lawrence? Not since they threw me out of Oceanique." He smirked. "Lost control of him, has she? She always was a controlling bitch. The poor man couldn't breathe without her making sure he was doing it the right amount of times per minute."

"Were you close to Lawrence?"

"That twat?" He chuckled. "No. He was a good boss – fair in the kitchen and better than most chefs – but as soon as I finished work, I went home." Then he frowned. "Why are you asking me about Lawrence? I didn't have anything to do with him, really, and I haven't since I got kicked out."

"Why did you get kicked out?"

Robbie sat silent for a moment. "I take recreational substances sometimes. Nothing serious, just low-grade stuff like everyone. Except one night before my shift I took what

I thought was just something to keep me alert. Turns out it wasn't what I thought it was and it gave me hallucinations."

Angus didn't think it was worth arguing that not everyone did drugs. In Robbie's world, perhaps everyone did.

Angus noted that Lydia had said Robbie was sacked because of stealing. Yet here he was telling a different story. "How did you feel about being sacked for that?"

Robbie shrugged. "It was annoying. I was learning a lot. Lots of people want to work at Oceanique for the prestige. Looks good on your CV."

"So you must have been resentful when you got sacked for something that wasn't really your fault?"

"Yeah, I was."

"Did you go back to the restaurant and have it out with them?"

"What? No, course not. No point, is there? Once you're sacked, that's it."

"Another member of the staff said you'd been hanging about outside the restaurant because you were upset at your sacking."

Robbie stared at him. "Who said that? Who is it? Tell me, and I'll sort them out." He smacked his fist into his palm.

"I can't tell you, and please don't get angry. I just want to know if you've been near the restaurant since they sacked you."

"I walk past sometimes because it's on the esplanade. That's it. They don't own the seafront, last I heard."

"How often?"

Robbie shrugged. "Dunno. Why?"

"Have you been hanging around the restaurant, then?"

"No," Robbie answered quickly.

There was a long silence between them. Angus stared at Robbie, assessing him. "And you haven't seen or heard from Lawrence since you were sacked?"

"Told you, didn't I? No. Why would I?"

Angus sighed thoughtfully. "All right. One more thing. Was there anyone at the restaurant you didn't get on with?"

"You mean, who would lie about me hanging round like a bad smell? Can't think of anyone." Robbie looked into space. "You know, you work with all sorts of people, you think they're all right, and then they do something like this. You can't trust anyone these days. Tell me who it was."

Angus shook his head. "I'm afraid I can't divulge who's told me what. It's part of my job to sift through the information I'm given and work out what's the truth and what's a lie."

"Well, I ain't got time to hang round Lawrence's gaff. I work here now and I'm doing extra hours. They're happy with my work here and I'm happy with them."

The server came over to the table. "Rob, they need you in the kitchen. Just had an order for two poached eggs."

Robbie stood up. "Gotta go."

"Thank you for talking to me," Angus said. He wanted to add that he believed Robbie but held back. For some reason, he thought Robbie was telling the truth. It was his intuition with no concrete evidence. Lydia's story was different, but Robbie had never hesitated when he'd told his side. It was all so inconsistent. For now, he'd work on the premise that Robbie was telling the truth, until other evidence, if there was any, came to light.

Chapter Twenty-One

"So Robbie hasn't been stalking Lawrence after all?" Charlotte said, once Angus had updated her later. They'd met up in Exmouth, near the restaurant.

"No. And he was quite put out when I suggested he might have been."

"Why would Lydia tell us that Robbie was stalking Lawrence when he wasn't?"

Angus shook his head. "And tell us he was Lawrence's dealer. I don't know, but she was quite emphatic about it, wasn't she? We need to talk to her again."

Charlotte got up. "Let's go."

But as they approached the restaurant, they saw a notice on the glass door: *Due to staff shortages, we are unable to open at lunchtime until further notice. We apologise for the inconvenience.*

Angus peered inside but couldn't see anyone. "I'll phone Cressida and ask where Lydia lives."

"What will you say when she asks why you want to talk to Lydia?" Charlotte asked.

"I'll say that we're speaking to all the staff and she's

next on the list. Lydia might have a valid explanation for her claim that Robbie was stalking Lawrence, for all we know."

They walked to a bench looking out to sea and sat down. Angus called, and when the call ended he had bad news. "It's Lydia's night off tonight and Cressida can't give us her address, as she hasn't got it."

"What? All employers are supposed to have their employees' address."

"She said Lydia moved recently and she hadn't told her the new one."

"I'll see what I can find out about Lydia online," Charlotte said. "I'm sure I'll be able to track her down."

Angus gave her an apprehensive glance.

* * *

Angus was vaguely aware of a phone ringing in the distance. It kept ringing, and he wished it would go away. Then it stopped.

He turned over in bed.

The phone rang again.

Angus scrabbled for it on the bedside table and looked at the display.

Charlotte.

He sighed, then pressed Accept.

"I've found her!" Charlotte cried, before he could say anything.

"What?"

"I've found her! Lydia. The server at Lawrence's restaurant."

"What time is it?"

"Four am."

"Charlotte, couldn't this have waited?" Angus rubbed his eyes.

"No, it can't! I've been tracking her on social media all night. She's been posting on Instagram about her night out. She started in a bar in Exeter, then went to a nightclub in Exmouth. She got out of there at two am and said she was going to Orcombe Point, but she hasn't posted again."

"Orcombe Point?" Angus knew it was a famous headland in Exmouth with a geoneedle, and a sharp drop forms the cliff into the sea. "Are you sure you've got that right?"

"Yes."

"That seems a strange place to go after a night out. Maybe she went home instead."

"Maybe. But it's strange. She'd been posting regularly all night until then. We should get over there."

Angus sat up in bed. "You want to go to Orcombe Point to see if Lydia's there?"

"Yes."

"Why not just wait until the morning and speak to her at home?"

"Because I'm suspicious. Why would she seek us out when we visited the restaurant and blame Robbie? Her story was inconsistent. I think she's up to something. Or worse – something has happened to her up there."

Angus sighed. "I guess seeing the sunrise at Orcombe Point won't be too bad."

"Great! Come over as soon as you can." And before Angus could argue, Charlotte ended the call.

* * *

When Angus drove up to the front door of Charlotte's house in Topsham, she appeared within seconds.

"Hello," she said, as she got in the car. The light which had come on when she opened the car door showed dark patches under her eyes.

"Have you been tracking her all night?"

"Yes."

The interior light went off.

"It'll be quicker to drive to the houses near the footpath to Orcombe Point, rather than the seafront path," Angus said.

"I agree. It should only take us five or ten minutes to get to the obelisk if we walk fast."

Angus set off. The early hour meant clear roads, and they arrived at Foxholes Hill ten minutes later. Angus pulled up at the side of the road, near the start of the footpath that led to Orcombe Point on the cliffs.

They got out of the car and gazed at the sea. They were high up on the cliff, and the sea was illuminated by an almost full moon. Behind them, the few bungalows were dark.

The path to Orcombe Point and the obelisk was a quarter of a mile long. They made their way along with the aid of a torch. Angus walked in front where there was only room for one, and the rest of the way, they walked side by side, both lost in their thoughts. After a few minutes, they could see the obelisk in the distance.

"I've never been here before," Charlotte whispered. "What's the obelisk for?"

"It's a marker for the western end of the Jurassic Coast," Angus replied. "When we get close, you'll see it's made of different types of stone from the local area."

Charlotte stopped when they were looking up at the tall pyramid structure, looming over them in the moonlight.

The gentle lapping of the waves below the cliff was the only sound.

Charlotte stared at it. "That's stunning."

"It's even better in the daytime. What are we looking for?" asked Angus. "Do you think this is a drugs drop? I think it's too remote and exposed for that. Wouldn't they just ship them to a dodgy house or garage?"

"Why would she mention Orcombe Point for no reason? There's nothing here except the monument and an amazing view of Exmouth and the English Channel."

Angus moved past the obelisk towards the cliff edge, while Charlotte read the plaque explaining its presence.

"The obelisk celebrates the twists and turns of our planet..."

"Charlotte."

"Deserts and seasons, evolutions and extinction were all recorded in layers of sandstone, clay and limestone."

"Charlotte!"

"It's a great way to show how the coastline from here to Dorset changes. I've never been interested in geology, but this could sway me."

"*Charlotte!*"

She looked over. "What is it?" she said testily.

"Come here. Please."

Charlotte walked towards Angus, then saw what was lit by his torch. "Oh my God!"

In front of them was a body.

Chapter Twenty-Two

Charlotte's hand flew to her mouth. "Shit!" She peered at the corpse. "Is that..."

"Lydia Harper. Yes."

"Oh my God! How... What? And she's been laid out that way on purpose."

Lydia lay on a brick compass circle, with north, south, east and west indicated by four triangles. Her legs pointed south, her arms east and west. In her forehead, a bullet hole.

"Who would do something so cruel?" Charlotte cried out.

Angus stood up and put his arm around her. Charlotte rested her head against his shoulder. "This is awful. How long do you think she's been dead?"

"I'm no pathologist, but my guess is not long. She's still warm. We need to call the police. I'll do it."

Charlotte raised her eyebrows. "Should you call my brother?"

Angus shook his head. "He's working on a case in north Devon at the moment. I'll go through nine-nine-nine. We need to be careful not to contaminate the area."

He let go of her, stepped back and dialled, trying not to remember that the last time he'd come across a dead body, he'd been arrested on suspicion of murder. It couldn't happen twice. And at least this time, the police officer attending would most likely be someone he knew.

Charlotte found her way to a bench and sat down. When Angus had finished, he came over to her.

"This has taken a sinister turn," he said. "It can't be a coincidence that Lydia is dead and Lawrence has gone missing."

"It's very suspicious. Do you think it's connected with Lawrence?" Suddenly she gasped. "Do you think Lawrence killed her?"

"It's a possibility: we can't rule him out. But this looks like a gangland killing rather than the work of a chef on the run. I'd have thought a knife would have been more his type of weapon."

Charlotte looked out to sea. "How long did the police say they'd be? There are rain clouds at Dawlish and they're coming our way."

Angus's gaze followed hers. The moonlight and the beginnings of dawn had made the sky lighter. "It might pass over the town rather than here. They'll send uniforms to cordon off the area and protect any evidence. I'd give them ten or fifteen minutes at least."

"What sort of evidence might there be?"

"Maybe whoever was up here dropped something."

Charlotte stood up. "Maybe we should look." She switched on her mobile phone torch and started to look around, moving carefully.

Angus stood up and did the same.

"What are we looking for?" she asked.

"Anything."

Five minutes later, they'd found nothing. Charlotte kept close to Angus as they searched.

Then Angus saw something a little way from the body.

"There ... look." He pointed to a rough area with long grass. He moved closer, put on a latex glove he took from his pocket and picked it up.

It was a mobile phone.

"Is it Lydia's?" Charlotte asked.

"I think so." He turned it over and they saw the bright pink-and-purple case.

"Hold on," Charlotte said. "Obviously the police will want it, but I can see what's on it." She tapped her phone and held it near Lydia's.

Angus raised his eyebrows. "What are you doing?"

"Copying everything that's on it."

"How?"

"I just need to press that button on the side. Do you have another glove?"

Angus moved the phone away. "That's interfering with evidence."

"No it's not. I'm just copying everything so we can look at it. I'm not changing anything."

"That's highly illegal."

"There's a highly illegal? How is that different from just illegal?"

Angus closed his eyes and shook his head. "Stop being facetious. You know what I mean."

"The program's untraceable. No one will know."

"I will!"

"Know what? I don't know what you're talking about. Nothing to see here." Charlotte smiled. "Come on. Give me the other glove. It'll take thirty seconds."

"I preferred it when you just hacked Wi-Fis."

"You said that a few days ago. Does that mean I can hack Wi-Fis now?"

Charlotte opened her bag and fished out her own latex gloves. She put them on, then held out her palm to Angus.

He paused. Then sighed and handed it over. She tapped the screen and it lit up. "There's no password on the phone. That's unusual. But it helps us, and it'll save time."

Angus couldn't watch. Charlotte shouldn't be doing this, he thought. But then again, it might help them crack the case. He scanned the path. The police would arrive any minute.

"Done," Charlotte said, a minute later.

"Just in time. I can see torches in the distance. The police are here."

Chapter Twenty-Three

Just as Angus had predicted, it was uniformed officers first.

"Do you know them?" Charlotte asked in a whisper as they approached.

Angus shook his head. "No, but I never worked in Exmouth. Plus, they look like they've just left school."

Charlotte couldn't help but smile. "They do look very young."

Charlotte stood back and let Angus deal with them.

They radioed through. Half an hour later, Angus's old sergeant, DS Simon Pearce, came with a detective constable.

The men shook hands, then Simon went over to Charlotte. "Miss Lockwood. It's been a while."

"It has. Hello, Simon. How are you?"

"I'm good. But I'll be better when I've drunk this." He held up a takeaway coffee cup.

"I was hoping you'd be the officer who came," Angus said.

"I happened to be on call. It's been a quiet week. Until

now. So, what have we here – and how did you come to discover this?"

"We've been hired to find Lawrence Westwood," Angus explained.

Angus nodded. "The TV chef who owns the restaurant on the seafront?" Simon asked.

"He's gone AWOL and his wife wants him found. It's affecting their business."

"I take it you don't think he's in danger."

"He's done it before: apparently he has some mental health issues. She wanted to keep it quiet to begin with. We've had a few leads, but nothing concrete yet."

"So what led you to Orcombe Point, and what has this woman got to do with it?"

"Her name is Lydia Harper. She works – worked – in Lawrence's restaurant as a server."

"You know her?"

"Not really: we met her once at the restaurant. She told us an ex-employee might be involved with his disappearance, that he'd been stalking Lawrence, but now we think she was lying. We're not sure why."

"Has anyone else visited the crime scene since you found her?"

Angus shook his head. "No, it's just been us."

Simon and Angus went over to the body. "Did you see anyone else here when you came?" Simon asked, crouching down for a closer look at the body.

"No one. We used the same path as you, but someone could have come and gone via the west route from the caravan park."

"Yes, that's right: you can get to Orcombe Point a different way. It's certainly possible."

"Might be worth checking to see if the caravan park have CCTV," Angus said.

"Thanks, I'll get someone to check that." Simon stood up. "Any idea why someone would want her dead?"

"No. Her death is a surprise."

"And what did you find when you checked him out?"

"Nothing."

"I'll need his name anyway. I'll check where he's been for the last few hours."

Angus wrote Robbie's name and address on his notepad, ripped out the sheet and gave it to Simon. "Robbie works at the budget hotel on the seafront. I don't think he's involved. I'm not sure why Lydia told us about him, but whatever reason she had, it's proved to be her downfall."

"You think it's connected?" Simon asked.

"Yes. This is too much of a coincidence."

Simon's eyes narrowed. Angus recognised that reaction. He wondered if he was annoyed that Angus was first on the scene, or miffed that he was being given advice. Maybe it was a bit of both.

"All right, I'll make a note to look into it." Simon looked over to where Charlotte was. "I need to wait for forensics. I'll see someone takes your statement."

Chapter Twenty-Four

Angus walked over to Charlotte, who was still sitting on the bench. She was frowning at her tablet computer. "Simon wants us to give statements," he said. "He's sending a PC later today."

Charlotte looked up from the tablet. "More statements." Then she looked over at Simon a short distance away, talking to a uniformed officer.

"You should know the drill by now."

"Oh, I wasn't complaining. It's just time-consuming." She switched off the computer. "I was just checking whether the caravan park beside the west route here has CCTV, but I couldn't find out. I need to get closer to their Wi-Fi."

"We could get closer," Angus said. "Then you could see if they have Wi-Fi."

"Is this your way of saying I can hack them?"

Angus smiled. "Or we could ask."

"There is that. But if they do have Wi-Fi, they're unlikely to tell us."

"If you don't ask, the answer's always no."

Charlotte looked at her watch. "It's seven o'clock. Most office workers won't start until nine, at least. I could have their public Wi-Fi and router hacked in the time it takes us to drive there and park nearby."

Angus looked out to sea. "Go on, then."

"Excellent. Let's go!"

The caravan park was the largest in East Devon. It was owned and run by a large national holiday company, and the road leading to it was tree-lined and long. Angus parked the car close enough to the entrance barrier, complete with security guard, for Charlotte to access the Wi-Fi signal, but far enough away that the guard wouldn't wonder what they were up to.

As soon as Angus switched off the engine, Charlotte took out her tablet computer and located their public Wi-Fi.

"They also have a private staff Wi-Fi," she told Angus. "That's the one to go for."

She tapped at the screen and Angus glanced at it, then away. It was still gobbledygook to him. Part of him wondered whether they should have just asked. Or they could have walked along the path to the caravan park to see if the park had CCTV, but that would have taken time. His stomach rumbled.

"We can get some breakfast once I've done this," Charlotte said, still engrossed in the screen. "Hopefully it won't take long. I've just found a list of passwords from the national company on the dark Web. I tried a few and hey, presto, I'm in!"

"Is there anything that isn't leaked on the dark Web?" asked Angus.

Charlotte looked up and smiled at him. "I don't think so."

Angus's eyes narrowed. "How much of *my* information is on the dark Web?"

"Not much. Login details to some websites you've signed up for."

"Is that all?"

"You got off lightly: anyone can tell you don't like tech. But you should definitely improve your passwords. They're short and easy to crack."

"Yes, well, anyway... Now you're in their network, have they got CCTV on the path from the caravan park to Orcombe Point?"

Charlotte tapped the screen. "Give me a moment..."

It was a few minutes before she spoke again. "They don't have CCTV there. There are a few cameras around the restaurant, but none point that way. So even if Lydia's killer did come via the caravan park path, there's no way we'll see them on a camera."

Angus turned the ignition key. "Well done, though it's not the answer we wanted. Let's get some breakfast."

They stopped at a café in the town centre. Angus ordered a full English and Charlotte got poached eggs on toast. They sat at one of the outside tables looking out over the town square.

"She can't have been more than twenty-five years old," Angus said. "She had her whole life ahead of her."

Charlotte nodded.

"She's not much older than my daughter. I don't know what I'd do if anything happened to her."

"I'd love to meet her properly."

Angus smiled. "When Grace isn't at uni, she's either travelling or busy."

"Doesn't she ever go up to Scotland and stay with your

parents? Or I'd have thought that as it's the summer holidays, she'd spend some time with you, at least."

"This summer she's been too busy, seeing friends and travelling."

"No boyfriend?"

"There was one for a while. But not at the moment."

Charlotte sipped her coffee. "I need a bucket of this. I got no sleep last night."

"After breakfast I'll drop you home, and you can get some shut-eye."

While they waited for their order to arrive, Angus called Cressida and gave her an update. When the call ended, he relayed what Cressida had said. "She says she's shocked. She had no reason to think that Lydia was involved with anything dodgy."

"Maybe Simon and his minions will find out if Lawrence's disappearance is connected."

"True." Angus smiled. "Sometimes I forget I've left the police. My inclination was to start directing everyone at the crime scene."

Charlotte grinned back. "You can take the uniform away from the man, but you can't take the man out of the uniform. Or something like that."

Angus chuckled.

Charlotte turned her coffee cup on the table. "You still do things you'd have done in the police. Whenever you leave a voice message, you always give the time and where you are, just like you're reporting into the police station."

Angus sat back in his chair with a quizzical look. "I do, don't I?"

"Mark does it too."

Their food arrived and they tucked in. A few minutes later, Angus's phone dinged. It was a text, from Cressida.

Lawrence just called. Come to the restaurant straight away.

They bolted the remainder of their food and went straight to Oceanique.

"What did he say?" Angus asked Cressida, as soon as they'd sat down in the restaurant. Cressida looked agitated and pale. That didn't bode well.

"I recorded it like you said, with that app." She unlocked her phone and pressed play.

"Hello?" said Cressida's voice from the recording.

Then they heard Lawrence's. "Cressida, it's me, Laurie."

"Lawrence! Where are you?"

"I'm scared, Cressida. I wanted to keep you out of it, but they're after me and now Lydia is dead. I didn't mean to do it. But I had no choice."

"What do you mean?"

"I'm sorry. They were after me and I had to do it."

"Who's after you? Please come home, Laurie. We can sort it out: you know we always do."

"I can't talk now. I'm in too deep to come home. I'm sorry, Cressida. I love you."

The call cut off, leaving a heavy silence in its wake. Angus and Charlotte remained motionless, Lawrence's words hanging in the air between them.

"Could you play it again?" Charlotte asked, eventually.

Cressida pressed play and the call repeated.

Angus rubbed the back of his neck. "You're sure it's him?"

Cressida nodded. "It was him. And he's pretty much admitted to killing Lydia." She sagged forward, buried her head in her arms and started crying.

"I need a copy of the recording from the app," Charlotte murmured, once Cressida's sobbing had slowed.

Eventually, Cressida lifted her head. "I can't hide this from the police. I won't become an accessory to murder, not even for my husband. God, Lawrence is such an idiot. How the hell did he get himself into all this trouble?"

"You need to call the police and let them have the recording," Angus said.

"We can do it for you," Charlotte said. "Angus knows the investigating officer."

Cressida sighed. "Whatever you think is best. It'll be all over the news soon enough, but we can try to hide it for as long as possible."

A missing chef, and a murdered girl who had worked at his restaurant, thought Angus. The gutter press will have a field day.

"The best thing to do is keep this out of the press as much as possible," he said. "Don't speak to anyone about it."

"I'll analyse the data from the phone call and see what I can find," Charlotte said.

Cressida looked puzzled. "What can you find from a phone call?"

Charlotte shrugged. "Maybe nothing, but I'll look anyway."

Chapter Twenty-Five

A ngus took Charlotte home, where she set to work analysing the data from the phone call.

"The number came through a VOIP app, which is good," she said. "That means I can find the IP address of wherever it originated."

"Really?"

"Yes. If Lawrence had called via the cellular network – so, a normal phone call – we'd have to try and get the originating call number from the phone company. As you'll know, that's almost impossible. But the call Lawrence made was through a VOIP app: Voice Over Internet Protocol, like WhatsApp or Skype. They use the internet. The call comes in through the data, and that means an IP address." Angus raised his eyebrows. "Sorry, an Internet Protocol address."

Angus shook his head, exasperated by the techno-babble. "So what have you found out?"

"That the call came from an IP address in South Devon."

"Can you pinpoint the exact location?"

"Pretty much. It's Newton Abbott." It was a town north

of Torquay and south of Dartmoor. Known for its industrial estates and businesses."

"Let's go, then." Angus picked up his jacket.

Charlotte shook her head and he paused, a look of surprise on his face. "But ... I don't think that was actually Lawrence speaking."

Angus's eyebrows knitted. "What do you mean? Cressida said it was him."

"I know, I know. But I think it was AI generated."

"Okay... Can you explain that to me without using any acronyms?"

Charlotte grew excited. "Sure. I analysed the audio because it sounded a bit strange. Not quite right, somehow. I think someone has used Lawrence's voice to train an AI voice generator and got it to say those things to Cressida."

Angus exhaled slowly. "Someone's trained AI?"

"Yes. The technology is amazing. You can train AI with a few minutes of someone's voice, and it will mimic it. Lawrence has been on TV more than enough times for someone to use a few of his programmes to train an AI voice generator."

"You can really do that?"

"Yep. It's been around for a while."

"But my bank keeps hassling me to move to voice recognition when I log into online banking!"

Charlotte gave a brief, dismissive shake of her head. "Don't do that unless you want to get hacked."

"I guess I've dodged a bullet there, then. Please, Charlotte, explain why you think it's AI so that even I can understand."

Charlotte turned the computer round. "This program can detect AI audio. It says there's a ninety-eight percent chance that the voice we heard on the call was AI, rather than a real person. Mainly because of the cadence of the voice."

"Okay..." Angus sat silently, taking this in. "How accurate is that thing?"

"Pretty accurate. As AI advances it might not stay so accurate. But for now, I reckon we need to work on the assumption that it's right."

Angus picked up his phone. "I'm going to call Cressida and ask her again if she's sure it was him."

He dialled her number and she picked up straight away. "Hi, Cressida, Angus Darrow here. Did you notice anything strange about Lawrence's voice when he called?"

There was a a long pause. "Well, he didn't sound himself, exactly. He sounded a bit ... odd."

"Can you say why that was?"

"Not really. He didn't sound himself, but if he'd just murdered someone, that's not surprising." She sighed. "Have you told the police about the call yet?"

"Not yet. We..." Angus wondered how to phrase his next words. "We think it might not have been him on the phone."

"An impersonator? Well, now you say that, it could have been..." Cressida sounded as if a burden had been lifted. "God, I hope so." A pause. "I honestly can't function at the moment. The whole world seems to be caving in."

"We're going to hold off on telling the police for the moment, but we can't do that for too long. We're going to investigate something first which should help us decide whether that call was real or fake."

"Please keep me posted," said Cressida.

Angus ended the call and turned to Charlotte. "We need to visit wherever that IP address is based."

Chapter Twenty-Six

I t took half an hour to get to Newton Abbot, where the IP address originated from. Charlotte directed Angus until they arrived at a brick office building that looked like it it had been built in the eighties. A sign outside said CWDomestic and Care Services.

Angus parked a little farther down the road, then turned to Charlotte. "Why would a domestic services' company in a town twenty-five miles away send an AI phone call to the wife of a TV chef to say that he's murdered one of his staff?"

"I'll double-check this is the right place. But yes. If this is where the call originated, what has all this got to do with them? And why do they want Cressida to think Lawrence has murdered Lydia?" She opened her laptop and pressed a few buttons on the keyboard. "Yep, the call definitely came from here."

"Then what has a domestic services business got to do with the disappearance of a TV chef and the murder of a member of his staff?"

"We need to go in and find out."

"We need a reason to go in, though," Angus said. "Have a look at their website. If they provide domestic and care services, they're bound to want employees all the time." Charlotte tapped at the keyboard. "You're right: they're looking for all types of domestic workers to be carers, cleaners, gardeners..."

"The sort of work which has a high turnover of employees."

"So what should we do?"

Angus looked at the building. "We know that the fake call pretending to be Lawrence came from in there, so we need to get inside and find out who was responsible. Can you do that?"

Charlotte crossed her arms. "It might take a while, and I'd need to get into their network. I can try and hack their Wi-Fi."

Angus gave her a sidelong glance. "Do it."

Charlotte didn't argue, she just typed at the screen. After a few minutes, she looked up at Angus. "I don't think they have Wi-Fi."

Angus stared at her. "No Wi-Fi?"

Charlotte grimaced. "I know! Strange, but they must have a wired network."

"I'd ask how you know that, and how you knew the phone call came from here, but you'll just come out with techno-babble."

"They don't have a Wi-Fi, which means they're using a wired network. Physical cables are *much* more secure and stop people like me from hacking them. I suppose I should give them credit!"

"Can you get access to the network?" Angus asked.

"Yes, but I'd need to get inside and tap into the cables. It's harder, but not impossible. I've infiltrated buildings before, you see. It's one of my favourite things about pen testing."

"Pen testing?"

"Penetration testing. It's a job title now, you know. People get paid huge amounts of cash to get into buildings and hack their networks. It's fabulous. I loved doing it before I sold my company. I didn't get to do it as much as I wanted to, though: I had to delegate a lot. Always too many management meetings."

"So you got paid to break into buildings?" He wasn't sure how he felt about that.

"Yep. It was all above board. Companies can only get insurance against cyber attacks if they get certificates from companies like mine which show they have at least some protection." Charlotte looked out of the car window. "Anyway, how will we get in there? We could be researchers studying the economic impact of domestic services in the region. We could say we're from a university ... or we could be IT consultants. That's easy to do, but these days people are more aware of being scammed." Charlotte tapped her finger on her lips. "I know! We could pretend to be routine maintenance. We've been hired to perform routine checks on something like the gas supply."

"No, we won't do any of that," Angus said. "We'll introduce ourselves and ask."

"Did you ever go undercover when you were in the police?"

"No."

"I can tell." Charlotte turned to face Angus, looking amused. "I know you like to tell the truth and do everything above board, but sometimes, in order to get to the truth, you need to fib a little."

"I don't lie."

"All right. Not lying, but hiding the truth. Anyway, *you* pretended to be from the council when we were on our first case and we thought someone we were looking into had kidnapped a boy."

Angus shook his head. "That was you, not me: I just kept quiet because I didn't want to let the cat out of the bag." He sighed. "All right, then. The most effective way to get in would be to pretend one of us is looking for work."

Charlotte raised an eyebrow. "One of us?"

"I'm not sure it's realistic for both of us to go in."

Charlotte smiled. "We could pretend we're married!"

Angus looked her up and down. "You look too smart and wealthy to want work as a domestic helper."

"And you're in a suit even though you were up before the crack of dawn," Charlotte countered.

"Why wouldn't someone after maintenance or domestic work wear a suit?" Angus adjusted his tie.

"It's just not the expectation, so you'll look odd. We need to rough ourselves up a bit."

Angus rolled his eyes. "How exactly can we do that when we're nowhere near home?"

"Take your jacket and tie off and mess up your hair."

Angus gave her a look that conveyed that was the last thing he'd ever do.

"Here." Charlotte leaned over and ruffled his hair.

Angus glared at her. "Honestly, Charlotte, I swear that if you ruffle my hair like that again, it'll be the end of our working relationship." He ran his hand through his hair, straightening it out.

"What are you, the Fonz from *Happy Days? Don't touch the hair,*" she said, impersonating Henry Winkler. Then she delved into her handbag. She pulled out an eyeliner pencil and added a thick line to her lower lids, then put on bright red lipstick. She pulled her hair into a pony-tail on top of her head, took off her jewellery and looked at herself in the mirror.

"Not bad: it'll have to do. We'll see if they have any jobs and have a general look round. Being up all night helps to give me a rougher-than-normal look."

They got out of the car and made their way to the build-ing, whose ugly eighties' features were even worse close-up. They went through the main entrance and into the empty reception.

They exchanged glances. Angus nodded, and they went farther into the building.

The corridor was quiet, and as they walked along, Char-lotte glanced into an office. Inside, a woman sat at a desk. Angus moved farther down and peeped into another office. This one was empty. He beckoned Charlotte inside and waited in the doorway, looking out.

Charlotte pulled out her tablet computer and a network cable, then put one end of the cable into the back of one of the computers and the other into her laptop to connect them up. "Let's see if I can plant my software." She tapped her screen a few times, then smiled. "As easy as taking sweets from a baby." She put the network cable back into the computer on the desk.

"Someone is coming." Angus whirled around and placed himself in the doorway.

Charlotte glanced up, then tapped at the laptop. "Come on. Why are computers so slow when you need them to be fast."

"Charlotte..." Angus pleaded.

"Can I help you?" The woman approached Angus. She was in her thirties, short, wearing a navy skirt suit.

"Hello." Angus hoped she wouldn't look in the room.

"Hi," Charlotte said, moving around Angus. "We were wondering if you had any vacancies? We're looking for work."

The woman looked Charlotte up and down. "Everything's done online now. You go to our website and fill in the form, then someone will contact you."

Charlotte gave Angus a sidelong glance.

"Donna!" called a woman's voice. "We need you out back. One of the girls is refusing to go to Mr Baxter's again. She says he's a rude old codger and she'd rather paint the Forth Bridge with a toothbrush."

Donna sighed. "All right. I'll just show these two out and I'll be right there." She turned to Charlotte and Angus. "This way, please."

They followed Donna to the exit, where she made sure they left.

"I'm definitely going to try and hack their website," Charlotte said, when they were back in the car.

Angus raised his eyebrows. "Why didn't you do that before we went in there?"

"Most non-tech companies like this use a third-party provider, but you never know. It's worth looking at."

"Fine. I'll drive you home, and then you can hack away to your heart's content."

Chapter Twenty-Seven

When Angus got home, he went for a run to clear his head of the accumulated technical jargon. After a shower, he called Simon for an update.

"No Charlotte with you?" Simon asked.

"No, she's busy on the case. What's the latest on the murder?"

"The cause of death was as we thought: a single gunshot to the head. The time of death was between two and four am: so possibly as little as a couple of hours before you found her."

"Any sightings of suspects?"

"No, none. We're looking through the CCTV from the town, but it's unlikely we'll find anything. If they came along the esplanade, we might see them, but the residential streets don't have anything. We'll put out a request for video doorbell evidence from homeowners nearby, but I'm not hopeful."

"They didn't come via the caravan park, then?" Angus

already knew the answer, but he wanted to see if the police had got any further.

"If they did, we wouldn't know, because the caravan park doesn't have CCTV near the path to Orcombe Point."

"Have you spoken to Cressida Westwood yet?"

"Not yet, but I'll be speaking to her in the next couple of days."

"About that... It seems that someone is trying to frame Lawrence for the murder."

"Really? What makes you think that?" Simon's voice was full of surprise.

"This morning, Cressida received a phone call from Lawrence where he implied he murdered Lydia. Luckily, Cressida had recorded it using an app on her phone. Charlotte analysed it and worked out that it was almost certainly AI generated. Someone spoofed his voice, and they're trying to blame him for Lydia Harper's murder."

There was a moment of silence, then a deep sigh. "Is Charlotte sure?"

"She is, and I've learnt to trust her completely on anything to do with computers and technology."

"I take it Lawrence is still missing?" said Simon.

"Yes. But I'm starting to think that he may be in trouble. And something's very wrong if someone is trying to frame him for murder."

"What did the message say?"

"That he didn't mean to do it and 'they' were after him. Nothing explicit stating he did it, but it was heavily implied. I'll get Charlotte to forward it to you, but remember, it's not him."

"All right. This is getting very messy."

"Murder's always messy," Angus replied.

"And does Charlotte know who sent the message?"

"She's working on that now."

"Thanks, Angus. Look, I have to go, but I mean it. Make sure you tell me anything else, however small, that might be relevant. Keep me up to date."

"I will."

* * *

The next morning, Angus returned to Charlotte's house to find out what she'd discovered.

Helena greeted him at the door. She was dressed in activewear: yoga leggings and a short top. "How are you?" She smiled.

Angus stepped inside. "Good, thanks."

Helena grabbed Angus's arm. "I arrive zis morning and find Charlotte asleep at desk," she whispered loudly. "What is zis case you are working on?"

"She hasn't told you?"

Helena shrugged. "She no tell me everyzing."

"We're trying to find a TV chef who's gone missing. Then this morning we found the body of one of his serving staff."

Helena gasped. "Another murder! Zis country, it supposed to be safe. Sometimes I think I go back to Romania."

A voice came from the lounge doorway. "If you do, I'll kidnap you and bring you back!"

"Morning, Charlotte," called Angus.

Helena put her hand on her hip. "You need to stay away from all zis crime."

"That's very hard when we're private investigators," Angus stated seriously.

"I don't know. Life was simple before."

Charlotte appeared. "And I was a mess."

Helena tutted. "Says woman who fall asleep at desk."

"Lots of people fall asleep at their desk," Charlotte protested.

"I've never done that," Angus said.

Charlotte shot him a look, and Helena gave a satisfied nod.

Angus realised he was letting himself be drawn into an argument, and it would be safer for him to hastily retreat. "Let's go to the study and catch up, Charlotte. I take it you've been busy?"

That provided the distraction needed. Angus and Charlotte went into her study, and Charlotte sat down at her desk. "I had a look on the conspiracy websites, and most of it's absolute rubbish," she said. "Though occasionally they'll come up with something which sounds unreal but is actually true. There were lots of rumours about Lawrence having an affair with an unknown woman."

Angus sat in the chair opposite Charlotte. "Was it one rumour which got repeated? And then everyone believed it, even though it might not be true?"

"Maybe, but there were comment threads by different people. One person in particular said that they're close to Lawrence's girlfriend, and they said she wants him to leave his wife but he won't. They reckon that's because Cressida is the brains behind most of what Lawrence does. You'll need to check that with Cressida, to see whether she thinks it's true." Charlotte sighed. "I feel for her. If it's true, she'll be devastated."

"Is there anything to indicate who the woman is?" asked Angus.

"Not so far, but I'll keep looking. There were several threads on Reddit, but that's just a long-form version of

Twitter, or X if you must. Lots of jealous and spiteful people want to twist the knife and bring down anyone and everything. But I have other news!" Charlotte beamed at him.

Angus couldn't help smiling back. "Go on..."

"My virus at CW Domestic and Care Services has found the computer in the building that the AI call came from. It's mainly used by a woman called Olivia Irving. She's some sort of human resources or personnel manager there."

"What have you found out about her?"

"She's from Taunton originally, but lives in Lympstone."

"That's a few miles away."

"Yep."

"And – *and* – I had a look at her social media profiles and she knows Liz Morgan because they're friends on Facebook."

"Liz, with the yurts, in Wales?"

"The very same."

Angus whistled. "That's no coincidence."

They were staring at each other, digesting this information, when Charlotte's phone rang.

"Hang on a minute," Charlotte said, fishing the phone from her pocket. "Probably a scammer." Then her expression changed. "It's Kaylee."

She accepted the call. "Kaylee? Are you all right?" She put the phone on speaker.

There was silence for a few moments. "That girl who was murdered at Orcombe Point got involved in something dodgy."

"Do you know who killed her?"

"No. But there's nasty people behind it. They're bringing illegals in."

Charlotte's eyes widened. "They're people-smuggling?"

"I shouldn't have said anything. But they're nasty, real nasty. Don't get involved or you'll end up like Lydia."

"Why, what do you know? Kaylee? Hello?" Charlotte held the phone in front of her and frowned at it. "Damn it. She put the phone down."

"Did she really say people-smuggling?"

"Yes." She looked at Angus. "Do we believe her?"

Angus shrugged. "Why would she lie?"

"Maybe we should try and find her."

Angus shook his head. "Not yet. If Kaylee is involved in what's going on, that could put her in danger." He paused, thinking. "We need more information. Is Lawrence a victim, or is he involved in all this?"

Charlotte leaned back in her chair, her mind racing. Then she got up abruptly and walked over to the conspiracy board, now filled with photos of people they'd spoken to. "If Lawrence is involved in people-smuggling, that's a big leap from being a TV chef. Could he have been coerced into it? Blackmailed, maybe?"

"We're also a long way from Dover and the Kent coast-line, which is where you'd think most people smuggling would take place," Angus pointed out. "Although, thinking about it, while Kent and West Sussex would be where you'd expect trafficking, Devon would be ideal."

"How long does it take by ferry from here to France?"

"As the crow flies, the nearest port in France is Cherbourg. I'd guess it would take between seven to ten hours by boat."

"Do you remember when we went to Lawrence's boat?" Charlotte asked. "I found out it had recently been to a small town in France near Cherbourg. Do you think they might be bringing over migrants?"

Angus raised his eyebrows. "That's quite a leap."

"It's a possibility, though."

"Have a look at that website that tracks boats."

"I searched before and there was nothing unusual. The website showed a couple of trips to France in the last few months, but all the other trips were just a few miles into the English Channel, which suggested it was just fishing."

"Check it again," Angus said. "See what it's been doing in the last few days."

Charlotte nodded. Ten minutes later, she'd pulled up more data on Lawrence's boat. "It's been out to sea a few times, but the path it took just looks like fishing again. Look, it's zigzagging across the sea."

"It might be nothing – but we can't exclude it. It's possible this is why Lawrence disappeared. He could be in hiding from the gang, especially if he stumbled upon what they were doing. We need to tread carefully, Charlotte: this is bigger than our usual cases. People-smuggling is danger-ous. And if Lawrence is in trouble, we need to understand the full picture before we make a move."

Charlotte sighed, feeling the weight of the situation. "If only we could dig deeper into Lawrence's recent activities and look for something that might connect him to this. But he just doesn't use electronic devices enough."

"And why would he be in London?" asked Angus.

"Hiding from someone?"

"Well, what we can do is check out Olivia Irving in Lympstone." Angus got up. "Let's go now."

Chapter Twenty-Eight

"I've always liked Lympstone," Charlotte commented, as they drove into the village on the eastern shore of the Exe Estuary. The roads were lined with traditional thatched cottages, and other local shops and traditional pubs. It had a tranquil old-world feel of Devon in bygone years.

"It is very nice," Angus agreed. "The posh bit of Exmouth, and just down the road from Topsham."

"Terrible for parking, though."

"That's the problem when most of the houses were built before the invention of cars."

"How inconsiderate." Charlotte smiled.

"When Grace was a child," Angus said, "we'd take the train to Lympstone, walk along the coast to Exmouth, and get the train back to Exeter." Angus glanced at the satnav, which showed they were not far from Olivia's house.

A pang of jealousy went through Charlotte at the thought of Angus spending time with Rhona.

Angus pulled up near a row of neatly trimmed hedges in the quiet street. They had a clear view of Olivia's house, a quaint two-storey building with a charming, slightly over-grown garden.

"Looks peaceful enough," Charlotte murmured, scanning the house through a pair of binoculars.

"Too peaceful," Angus replied, his gaze fixed on the front door. He adjusted his seat for a better view. "Appearances can be deceptive, especially in our line of work. I bet there are all sorts of secrets and lies in a village like this."

"That's very cynical of you." Charlotte mused for a few moments. "She's like me. She lives in opulent surroundings, but according to the info I've found on her, she's just an ordinary working woman."

"Nothing wrong with that."

"I know, but..."

"Lympstone isn't cheap. Maybe she won the lottery," Angus speculated.

"Not as far as my research goes. If she works in admin, or even middle management, she must have had some windfall to be able to live here."

"What about husbands or exes?"

"None that I could find. There's not many photos of her. I could only find one social media profile of her, and that had no photos."

"Not even a profile picture?"

"No, just a photo of a landscape. Could be anywhere. Here is the only photo of her I could find so far."

Angus looked at the tablet computer. Olivia was stood in a staged photo outside a modern glass office building, her hand on her hip, smiling at the camera. She wore black trousers and an oversized pale-red blouse. She had short grey-blonde hair that had been smoothed down and a thick covering of makeup that made you wonder how bad she looked without it.

"In that photo, she's wearing a lanyard. I'll see if I can enhance the photo and find out where she was working."

"So maybe Olivia is bent in some way." Angus looked Charlotte in the eye. "I want you to hack her Wi-Fi."

Charlotte stared at him. "But—"

"Don't start on me. She's involved somehow. I know it."

Charlotte reached into her bag and pulled out her tablet computer, eager to start before he changed his mind. "Okay, let's see what I can do." She tapped at the screen. Angus continued watching the house.

"She's on the move," he said, ten minutes later. "She's getting into her car. We need to follow: hacking will have to wait."

Charlotte packed away her laptop as Angus started the engine. "Let's see where she's headed," she said, her eyes tracking Olivia's car as it moved off.

They followed at a safe distance as Olivia drove through the winding streets of Lympstone and out towards Exmouth. Eventually, she pulled up outside a house in the middle of town.

Angus parked a short distance away, and they watched Olivia get out and quickly glance around before hurrying to the front door. It was opened by a bulky man who nodded, then ushered her in.

"This doesn't look like a friendly visit," Angus observed. "Things have just got a lot more complicated."

They sat in silence, contemplating their next move. Something was going on – and whatever it was could well be the key to understanding Lawrence's disappearance.

Charlotte took out her computer again and typed. "I'm not hopeful they'll have anything to hack, but you never know."

"Before you hack the Wi-Fi, find out who lives here."

Charlotte searched for the address. "It says here it's someone called Michael Smith. That's a suspiciously ordinary name."

It was nearly an hour before Olivia reappeared, and Charlotte couldn't locate a Wi-Fi to hack. Olivia looked up and down the road, got back in her car and drove home.

"Do you think Lawrence is in that house she just left?" Charlotte asked, once Olivia had gone back inside.

"It's possible. It could be worth staking it out. But before that, I want find out what Liz Morgan knows about Olivia."

"Should we visit her in Wales again?"

Angus shook his head. "We'd be better to stay here and looking into that house. I'll call her."

Back at Charlotte's house, Angus called Liz and put his phone on speaker. She answered after a few rings.

"It's Angus Darrow," he said.

"Oh, hello. If you're calling to find out if Lawrence has been here, he hasn't." She sounded slightly out of breath.

"That's useful to know. But I'm calling about someone else: Olivia Irving."

"Olivia?"

"You know her?"

"Well, yes, of course I do. I used to work with her. Must be seven or eight years ago now. It was a company in Newton Abbott that supplied domestic and care staff. She still works there."

"Are you friends?"

"Yes, but we don't get to see each other much now that I live in Wales. What has this got to do with anything?"

"Does she know Lawrence?"

"She's met him. They met at my birthday party a few years ago. But I don't think they know each other beyond that."

"Are you sure?"

"I'm not their keeper. They might have contacted each other – but if they have, I know nothing about it." Her tone was belligerent.

Angus and Charlotte eyed each other. Angus shrugged.

"Has Lawrence ever mentioned Olivia to you?"

"I don't remember him talking about her, no." A pause. "But why are you asking me about Olivia?" Her voice was querulous. "Do you think she has something to do with Lawrence's disappearance?"

"We're not sure. But thank you for speaking to us."

"You should at least explain why you're asking."

"It's better we keep our investigation confidential at the moment."

Liz sighed. "I don't like it. But as I said, as far as I know, they only met once, at my fiftieth birthday party a few years ago. Do you think they're having an affair? Is that it? Because if they were, neither has told me, and well... Olivia's a lovely woman, but not Lawrence's type at all."

Charlotte raised her eyebrows, her expression a mix of surprise and scepticism. What would Lawrence's type be?

"Thanks again, and if you think of anything else that might connect them, please phone me straight away." Angus ended the call.

"Well? What do you think?" Charlotte asked, after a moment of silence.

"I think she was telling the truth – but I'm sure Lawrence and Olivia are connected in some way. They could be involved in something together, or she could be involved with his disappearance. We need to find out if Lawrence is at Olivia's house, and if not, check the house she visited in Exmouth."

"The man who let her in there looked fierce," Charlotte said, with a slightly apprehensive expression.

"We need to play it safe with that house," Angus replied. "Chances are that there are more like him inside. I'm going home to prepare for staking out Olivia's house."

"I'll come with you," Charlotte said.

"No, you stay here and see what else you can find out about Olivia and Lawrence. Maybe she's behind these affair rumours."

Chapter Twenty-Nine

When Angus got home, he had something quick and easy to eat, a bowl of pasta and pesto. Then he prepared to stake out Olivia's house. He found his digital camera, and was packing some food and drink when his doorbell rang. He looked at the clock: 6.00pm. Were his parents surprising him again?

But when he opened the front door, instead of his parents, two burly men stood there. Angus recognised one straight away: The man Olivia had visited in Exmouth.

"Evening," said the other, and stepped forwards.

He pushed Angus back into the hall. The other man came in, too, then closed the door behind him.

"You can't just barge into my house!" Angus said. He felt a rush of adrenaline. Two against one was unfair, and they looked like people who, when they weren't bursting into someone's house, were down the gym lifting heavy weights. They were both almost bursting out of their blue jeans. One wore a tight mustard-yellow T-shirt, the other a tight blue T-shirt with the words *Born to Lift*, with a little image of barbells. Their stance and bulk reminded Angus of a pair of gorillas.

"Where's the woman?" the blue one asked.

"Woman?" Angus tried to keep his expression deadpan.

"The woman you were with."

"I work alone," Angus said, flatly.

"Don't lie to me." The man gripped Angus's neck. "You were with a woman when you staked out Olivia."

Angus shook his head. "I told you, I work alone. Olivia's lying to you." He could just about squeeze the words out.

The man's eyes narrowed. I've got something, thought Angus. Olivia's lied to him before.

The man let go of his neck, then turned to his companion. "Search the house. See if you can find any sign of a woman." He turned back to Angus. "Where's your phone?"

"Who are you, and what do you want?"

The man chuckled. "You know exactly why we're here. You can't sniff around and not expect a visit."

"I'm looking for Lawrence Westwood. He's gone missing."

The man put his palm out. "Phone."

Angus reached into his pocket and handed him his phone.

"Unlock it." The man held the phone out.

Angus went to take it, but the man held on. He put his thumb on the button.

The man scrolled through Angus's call log. "Who's Charlie?"

Angus still hadn't changed the contact details on his phone from the first time Woody had given him Charlotte's name. "My best friend. He works in IT. One of those geeky types. Works for the Met Office."

The man eyed Angus, then put the phone in his pocket.

Angus heard a thump from upstairs and winced. The gorilla was clearly making a mess up there.

"Do you know where Lawrence is?" Angus asked.

"I ask the questions, not you."

Upstairs, the other gorilla reappeared. "Nothing up there, and no sign of a woman. Looks like he lives alone."

"Rub it in, won't you," Angus said, managing a weak smile.

The first gorilla grabbed Angus's arm. "Right, we're going. *Move.*"

They marched him out of the house to an SUV with blacked-out windows. Gorilla One got into the driving seat, while Gorilla Two manhandled Angus into the back seat and sat beside him. "Don't try anything stupid," he said, scowling.

Angus didn't bother to reply. He was too busy wondering what the men wanted and how he was going to get out of this one.

Chapter Thirty

The SUV drove out of Exeter and towards Exmouth. Several times, Angus's phone rang. It was Charlotte's ringtone – the first few seconds of "Independent Women" by Destiny's Child. He hoped the Gorilla One's intellect wasn't sufficient to wonder why a man would be given that ring tone. Gorilla One ended each call, and after the third he switched the phone off. That didn't bode well. Charlotte wouldn't be able to track his whereabouts with the phone switched off.

Angus had assumed the men would take him to the house they'd seen Olivia go into, but the SUV drove through Exmouth to the quay. They parked close to the boats. "Out," barked Gorilla Two. "And no funny business."

Angus got out and looked around. There was no one nearby, and he weighed up the risk of running for it. He was a fast runner, and he doubted either of the men would be. But Gorilla Two seized his arm in a vice-like grip and marched him down the gangplank of the nearest boat. Angus just managed to register the name: *Bistro Buoy*. Lawrence's boat.

Gorilla Two pushed Angus onto the bridge. Inside was Remy La Galle.

Remy looked up from the computer at the interruption. He stared at Angus, then the gorillas. "Why he here?"

"He's been sniffing around," Gorilla One answered.

"You idiot. You just needed to lay low for a while," Remy said. "We leave now."

"All right," Gorilla Two stated and handcuffed Angus to a handrail on the bridge.

"I'll need you to prepare ze deck below," Remy stated. "The bags need shifting. You both need to do it before we get to ze rendezvous point."

Gorilla Two nodded and left the bridge.

Remy turned to the controls and started the engine.

"Il y a une lourde peine de prison pour un enlèvement, tu sais," Angus stated. There's a hefty prison sentence for kidnap.

Remy didn't look round. "Seulement s'ils m'attrapent."

"I admire your optimism at not getting caught. But if you let me go, it wouldn't be kidnap," Angus replied.

"I'm sorry, I can't do zat."

Remy disappeared out of the cabin for a minute, then reappeared. Angus supposed it had been to untie the boat from the quay because Remy piloted the boat and Angus could feel the boat moving.

Charlotte looked at her phone and frowned. She'd tried calling Angus three times, and after the fourth time, the phone had gone straight to voicemail. She sent a text: *Call me as soon as you can*

It wasn't like Angus to ignore her calls for so long. She

clicked on the tracker app. The last location shown was on the A376, between Exeter and Exmouth: near the Lympstone turnoff.

"That's strange," Charlotte murmured. Something didn't feel right. If Angus was driving, why would he switch his phone off mid-journey? He would never break the law by touching his mobile phone while driving.

Maybe the battery had died.

No: Angus never ran out of charge. Something was definitely wrong.

Charlotte got up and started pacing. She needed to calm down. Of course Angus was all right. She was just jumping to conclusions and letting her imagination run away with her.

Her phone rang when she was halfway across the room and she ran back to it. Expecting it to be Angus, she was disappointed to see Kaylee's name on the display.

"Hello?" she gasped.

"That bloke you're with, they've got him." Kaylee's voice was almost a whisper.

"What? Angus? Who's got him?"

"They took him on a boat."

"Boat? Which boat?"

"That chef's boat."

"Where are you?"

Silence.

Charlotte's heart was thumping in her chest. "Where are you?" she repeated.

"Exmouth Quay."

"What are you doing there?"

"Just hanging around."

"Is the boat still there?"

"No, it's gone."

"Shit. Stay there, I'm coming."

Charlotte ended the call and grabbed the keys to her Volvo: there wasn't time to wait for Grigore. Then she paused, went into her storeroom and picked out some hacking equipment.

As she was driving towards Exmouth, she had a thought and stopped the car. If Angus was in trouble, she needed help.

She dialled Simon's number and he answered after four rings. "Miss Lockwood, how are you?"

"Angus is in trouble," she said, straight away.

There was a pause, then he said in surprise, "What?"

"I think a gang has taken him."

"Why? Where?"

"Exmouth. I'm on my way now."

"Er, Okay. Tell me what you know, and I'll get help."

For a moment, she wondered whether Kaylee had been lying. But Angus's phone had disappeared as though someone had switched it off.

She tried not to panic as she explained it all to Simon.

"I'll get some uniforms down there and meet you at the quay," he said, and rang off.

The journey to Exmouth seemed to take for ever. The traffic lights were all red, and there seemed to be far more vehicles on the road than usual.

Charlotte parked as close as she could to the quay. She was about to ring Kaylee when she appeared from round the side of a building. She was dressed in baggy jeans and a grey hoody, and her hair was in a scruffy ponytail. Charlotte took hold of her arm. "Tell me everything."

"There was two of them. They got him out of that car." She pointed to a black SUV.

157

Charlotte took a photo of the number plate with her phone and sent it to Simon.

Kaylee took out her phone and showed Charlotte a photo of Angus on the boat with two hulking men. One had hold of him.

"When did they leave?"

"About ten minutes ago."

Charlotte looked out to sea. "Did you hear them say where they're going?"

Kaylee shook her head.

Charlotte took out her tablet computer. "I can track the boat using its AIS system – assuming they haven't turned it off."

"What's that?"

"It's GPS, but for boats. There's a website where you can track any boat."

Charlotte tapped at her screen despite her fingers shaking a little. A map of the world appeared and she zoomed in on Exmouth. "They can't have gone far," she muttered, with concern. "There's the boat, see?" She pointed, and a small icon representing a boat came into focus. "It's heading into the English Channel. We have to get him back before they harm him."

Chapter Thirty-One

Angus reviewed his options. They were limited. Even if he could get the handcuffs off, jumping overboard wasn't on. He was a competent swimmer, but the cold would get to him before he reached shore. Even in the summer, the water was too cold to survive long. They were clearly heading into the English Channel. Maybe they were going to France.

At least the gorillas were leaving him alone, and Remy was busy sailing the boat. Angus looked around for something he could use, but with both wrists cuffed, there was little he could do. His only hope was that Charlotte would realise he was missing.

It was nearly an hour before the boat slowed. Then the engine stopped and Remy went on deck. It was almost dark outside: all Angus could see were lights from another vessel. It was only when they pulled up alongside that he could see it was a large yacht.

One of the gorillas came over to Angus and undid his cuffs. "Try anything stupid, I'll throw you overboard," he growled, as he turned the key. Angus tried to take comfort in that presumably the gorilla wasn't planning to throw him overboard, anyway.

As soon as the cuffs were off, the gorilla grabbed Angus's arm and marched him out on deck and over the gangplank to the yacht.

It took Angus's eyes a few moments to adjust to the brightness of the yacht. Then he blinked. About ten men of Middle Eastern origin were sitting on the deck.

"Take them," shouted a new gorilla. Gorilla Two nodded and told them to get up. They got to their feet, and Angus watched them board the *Bistro Buoy*.

So people-smuggling *was* at the heart of all this, he thought.

Then, from below deck, someone emerged.

Cameron Wright, the TV producer.

There was a palpable change in the gorillas' demeanour as he approached. Where there had been casual and relaxed postures earlier, there was now rigidity and silence.

He surveyed the fishing boat, not even glancing at Angus, then spoke to one of the crew, and the *Bistro Buoy* set off.

Then he turned around and saw Angus. His presence on the yacht came as no surprise. He walked over to him.

"You really should have left well enough alone. You have no idea what you're getting into." He gave a half smile.

"Where's Lawrence?"

"You have more things to worry about than Lawrence. What am I going to do with you? Now you know my secret, I can't let you go."

Images of Lydia Harper dead at Orcombe Point flashed through Angus's mind. "You're going to shoot me in the head, like Lydia?"

Cameron smiled again. "Possibly." Then his face

became serious. "Get him below decks. I'll deal with him later."

Gorilla Two turned to Angus. "Down there." He pointed to some steps leading below deck.

Angus considered what to do. He didn't know how to pilot a yacht, and he didn't know how many other people were on board. His chances of overtaking all the crew, were slim. For now, he'd have to do what they asked and try and think of a way to escape.

He went down the steps, followed by the gorilla. Inside were two doors. Gorilla Two opened the one on the left, shoved Angus in and locked the door behind him.

The room was dimly lit, but Angus could feel that he wasn't alone. He turned, and saw a dishevelled man in scruffy jeans and a T-shirt. A very familiar man.

"Lawrence!"

Chapter Thirty-Two

Charlotte phoned Simon again. "They've taken him out on Lawrence's boat."

"Any idea where?"

"No, but I'm tracking it. It's about two miles out."

"And you're sure he's on board?"

"I have a reliable witness and photographic proof."

"I'll alert the coastguard."

Charlotte ended the call and turned to Kaylee. "Do you know if there's anywhere I can hire a boat and a pilot?"

"There's a couple down there, but it's late. They've probably gone home."

"I have to try. Which way?"

Kaylee pointed and Charlotte raced along the dock, her eyes scanning every boat. To her dismay, the boats were either unattended or unsuitable for the task at hand.

All she could think about was Angus. What if he ended up as Lydia had, with a bullet in her head?

As Charlotte reached the end of the dock, her hope dwindling, she noticed a group preparing a boat for departure. It was a rigid inflatable, red and white, with a deep-V hull. *HM COASTGUARD* was emblazoned on the side. Charlotte ran to them and explained the situation as quickly as she could.

To her relief, the coastguard team was aware of Angus's predicament. "We've been briefed and we're ready to go in a few minutes," one of the officers told her. "We're just waiting for a police officer."

"Thank God! They've already killed a woman, and I'm worried they might kill Angus too."

"Try not to worry, love. I'm sure everything will be all right."

A siren wailed and got closer, then a police car pulled up. Simon got out of the passenger side and went straight to Charlotte. "I'll go with the coastguard. A police boat is being deployed but it's coming from Torquay."

"Torquay? That'll take for ever!"

"It's a fast one: it'll be here in no time."

"I hope they're armed," Charlotte said, feeling apprehensive. "I'm sure the people with Angus will have guns."

"The officers are armed," said Simon.

"We're all set to go," one of the coastguard team shouted from the boat a few minutes later. "You Detective Pearce?"

Simon moved closer. "Yes."

"Come on board and we'll sort you out with a life jacket."

Charlotte stepped forward. "I'm coming too." Charlotte stepped forward.

Simon looked at the boat, then at Charlotte's pleading face. "All right. Let's go."

They boarded the coastguard vessel, where they were given life jackets, and then the engine roared as they set a course for the open sea.

Charlotte stood on the deck, staring into the darkness,

determined to find Angus and bring him back safely. Her usual seasickness was wiped out by her anxiety for Angus.

Eventually, one of the crew shouted, "We're closing in. Should be within visual range soon."

Charlotte could just make out a faint dot ahead of them. "There." She pointed. "That must be Lawrence's boat."

As they drew closer, the outline of the boat became clearer. It was moving at a steady pace, unaware of the vessel behind it. The captain of the coastguard team manoeuvred the boat skilfully, closing the gap..

Gradually, they drew alongside. Once they were parallel to the *Bistro Buoy*, the coastguard vessel slowed, matching the speed. Charlotte's heart raced and her palms were clammy. The next few moments were crucial.

Simon stood with his hand on the radio transmitter. "This is it," he said, his voice steady but tense. "Let's find out what's going on here."

The captain turned the boat's floodlights on, illuminating Lawrence's boat with harsh, bright light. The sudden illumination caught the occupants of the fishing boat off guard, and they gaped at the new arrival.

Charlotte took a deep breath. The moment of truth was upon them, and there was no turning back.

A team member with a loudhailer faced the *Bistro Buoy*. "Stop your engine and let us board."

"There must be at least ten men on there. They're smuggling them in," Charlotte shouted in Simon's ear.

The fishing boat stopped. The coastguard boat moved closer, and an officer tied up the fishing boat with a stout rope. A gang plank was lowered.

Charlotte scanned the men on the boat. "I can't see him!" she shouted.

"I'll go and search," said Simon. He crossed the gang-plank, accompanied by two officers.

Charlotte continued to peer at the fishing boat. "Where are you, Angus?" she murmured.

Torches flashed, the sound of shouted questions carried over to her, then she saw Remy, and she felt a surge of disdain go through her at his previous lies. She could see Simon moving back and forth, speaking to those on board. As long as he was still looking, there was hope.

Then Simon looked back at her, and shook his head.

Chapter Thirty-Three

Lawrence stood up. The cabin was small and smelt of stale sweat. A pile of dirty plates sat on the floor. "Who are you?" he asked.

"My name is Angus Darrow. I'm a private investigator: your wife, Cressida, hired me to find you. How long have you been here?"

Lawrence ran a hand through his hair, which was tousled and greasy. He hadn't shaved for a while either. "A few days. They've been using my boat to smuggle illegal migrants over from France."

"Are they landing them in Devon?"

Lawrence sighed. "Yeah, they've been moving along the coast. It takes longer, as the distance from France is much greater, but they have free rein. No one's expecting migrants this far along the coast."

"How did you get involved?"

"That bitch Olivia made me do it. She seduced me, then did her best to ruin me."

Angus blinked. "Olivia's part of the gang, isn't she?"

"I didn't know that at the time, obviously. Cressy and I

166

have been going through a difficult patch. All work and no sex, and I got tired of being bossed around. Olivia understood me – or at least, I thought she did."

"You started the affair?"

Lawrence nodded. "It was just a casual thing – for me, anyway. It was exciting too. Sneaking around, hiding stuff, working out where and when we'd meet. I had something to look forward to when I got up in the morning. I hadn't felt like that for years."

Lawrence caught Angus's eye and shrugged. "You can judge me for that if you like. No doubt you will, as you're working for Cressy. But our marriage has been hanging by a thread for a few years now."

"All marriages have their problems."

"Cressy wouldn't listen when I told her I didn't want to open more restaurants. I liked doing the TV show and having the restaurant in Exmouth, but she wanted to conquer the world. The culinary world, anyway."

"What happened with Olivia?"

"I got into debt: Failed investments Cressy knew nothing about. But it turns out I should have listened to her. Olivia said she'd lend me the money, but it was just a way for her to get to use my boat."

You've been played like a fiddle, thought Angus. "I take it you could hide the smaller amounts from Cressida, but not that."

Lawrence put his head in his hands. "I told them I could get the money if they waited. But then they'd wipe the debt if they could use my fishing boat a few times. I asked them what they wanted it for, but they said that me knowing that wasn't part of the deal. I refused at first, but then they started to threaten us. Me and Olivia, I mean."

"So you let them use the boat?"

Lawrence closed his eyes for a moment. "They even installed their own skipper."

"Remy?"

"Yeah."

"When did you work out what they were doing?"

"Not long after it started. At first, I thought they were bringing in drugs." He gave a bitter laugh. "Olivia told me in the end, after an argument. She said they'd been forcing her to filter the migrants through her work agency."

"She set you up?"

"She did, the bitch. She said her feelings for me were real, but I don't believe her."

"What about Cameron?"

"They're in it together."

Silence fell as they thought this over. Eventually, Angus said, "I suppose a fishing boat is less suspicious than a yacht like this."

"It is. They land the people at night a bit farther down the coast."

"How long has this been going on?"

Lawrence shrugged. "About six months. When I found out what they were doing I told them I wanted out., but they told me there wasn't a way out. Once I was in, that was it."

"Where did they keep you before here?"

"France at first; they've got houses there. I said I was going to the police, you see. They couldn't decide what to do with me."

Angus suppressed a sigh. Telling a gang he was going to the police was the last thing Lawrence should have done. But it was too late to undo that now.

Suddenly, Lawrence leaned towards him. "I think

they're going to kill me," he whispered. He burst into tears and his whole body shook.

Angus moved closer to Lawrence. "I think they're planning on killing us both. They've already murdered Lydia."

Lawrence looked up at Angus. "What?" He looked genuinely horrified.

"She was involved, too, wasn't she?"

"Yes. They made me take her on in the restaurant. She helped look after the migrants when they arrived."

"Can you think why they killed her?"

"She wanted out too. I could tell: she was always on edge."

"Did you speak to her about it?"

"No. I didn't know if I could trust her, not really. But she seemed vulnerable, you know?"

"They cloned your voice with AI and put a call through to Cressida where you admitted you'd killed her," Angus said. "My guess is that they're planning to make your death look like suicide."

Lawrence stared at Angus, fear in his eyes. "The bastards!"

"Why were you in the flat in London?"

"I went there just after I'd told Cameron I wanted out. Then they threatened me and I ran. I made the mistake of meeting up with Olivia. She said she'd help me, but she must have told them where I was. That's when they grabbed me." He shook his head.

"We need to act fast. How many men are on board?"

"I don't know." Lawrence seemed sunk in despair.

Angus looked around the cabin. There was nothing in it except for dirty plates.

Angus picked up a knife and fork and put them in his pocket. "I'm not going down without a fight."

Soon afterwards, the cabin door opened. One of the gorillas stood there. "Come out."

"I'm not going out," said Lawrence. "You're going to kill me."

The gorilla sighed. "No we're not. We've got work for you."

Angus stood up: it was now or never. "Come on, Lawrence. You heard the man: they have work for us. We can't hide in here for ever." Angus felt a wave of nervousness go through him, but he was running on adrenaline and he wasn't going to give up without a fight.

The gorilla grunted.

Angus gave Lawrence a look and he got to his feet. They left the cabin and followed the gorilla onto the deck.

Chapter Thirty-Four

O n deck, Gorilla One went to stand with Gorilla Two.

"What do you want us to do?" Lawrence asked. His voice shook.

The gorillas looked at each other, then the one in the blue T-shirt took out a knife and showed it to Lawrence. "You need to prove your loyalty." He glanced at Angus, then back to Lawrence. "Kill him."

"What?" Lawrence stared at the knife. Angus recognised the handle: the missing knife from Lawrence's London flat. "No! I won't do it!"

"They'll kill you anyway, Lawrence. They've already framed you for Lydia's murder."

Gorilla One's eye twitched. "How do you know that?"

Angus shrugged. "It was obvious, when I analysed the audio. And I know it came from Olivia's computer at CW Domestic."

"I hate her!" Lawrence said.

Gorilla Two flexed his shoulders. "Take the knife, or you'll both go over the side."

Lawrence spoke up. "If you're going to kill me anyway, you'd better get on with it."

Gorilla One shook his head regretfully. "It would have been much easier for you if you'd just done what we asked."

Just then, a light flashed in the distance. "What the—" muttered Gorilla Two. Then it flashed again.

Angus saw his chance. The gorillas were much bigger and stronger than he was, but he wasn't going to let them take him – no matter who was in the distance. With a grunt, he launched himself at Gorilla One, and his shoulder slammed into an iron midriff.

They hit the deck in a tangle of limbs and the knife flew out of the gorilla's hand. Angus threw a punch which connected with the side of the man's head, but he retaliated with a knee to the ribs. Angus felt the air rush out of him, but he wasn't backing down. He swung again and caught his opponent's jaw.

The two men rolled on the deck, each trying to gain the upper hand. Gorilla One managed to get on top and aimed a punch at Angus's face, but Angus jerked away, taking a glancing blow instead of a direct hit. He shoved at Gorilla One's shoulders, trying to dislodge the heavier man.

As they struggled, the light flashed again, closer this time.

"Lawrence, don't just stand there," Angus gasped.

"What do I do?"

The other gorilla looked at Lawrence. "Don't you do anything," he muttered.

All of a sudden, Lawrence lunged for a red-and-white life jacket and with a mighty swing, whacked it into Gorilla Two. It sent him staggering backwards.

That was all Angus needed. As the man on top of him watched his colleague retreat, Angus summoned the last of his strength and delivered an uppercut to the man's chin which made him recoil. He pushed him off and was about to punch him again when he saw a thick rope connect with the man's head. The gorilla's eyes rolled back and he slumped on the deck, unconscious.

Lawrence stood over him, panting, the rope swinging in his hand. The other gorilla stared at the man splayed out on the floor.

Another flash of light. Angus looked round and saw a red-and-white boat. Then a loudhailer crackled into life. "This is the coastguard. Prepare to to be boarded. Repeat: prepare to be boarded."

Chapter Thirty-Five

Still with *Bistro Buoy*, Charlotte looked and tried not to panic at the thought of Angus floating somewhere in the sea.

"These men weren't on the boat when it set off from Exmouth, and it hasn't had time to land anywhere else. This boat must have met up with another one."

One of the coastguard team checked the radar. "There's a boat about two miles north. Nothing else could have come close enough in the time they've been out. We'll head towards it."

The speed and rocking motion of the boat should have made Charlotte sick, but all she could think about was Angus. If he wasn't on the other boat, she wasn't sure what she would do. She thought about his parents. How could she tell them what had happened?

Charlotte stood on the deck of the coastguard's boat, peering through binoculars at the yacht.

She hardly dared to hope. What if Angus wasn't there? What if she got her hopes up and they were dashed? But she kept the binoculars trained on the deck as the boat lurched towards the yacht.

Two men were standing over another man, who was lying on the deck. One of the standing men had Angus's build. Could it be...? She hoped against hope that he wasn't the man on the deck. Although, if he was, hopefully they'd come in time...

The man with Angus's build looked round and her heart leapt. It was Angus! And now she could see that the man beside him was Lawrence.

Charlotte didn't wait to be asked to board; she followed the others onto the gangplank as soon as it was down. The coastguard and Simon, ahead of her, hailed Angus and Lawrence. Then Angus spotted her and his face lit up. "Charlotte!" he cried.

"Angus! Oh God, I thought they'd killed you!" She threw herself at him and wrapped her arms around his neck. He clasped her around the waist and pulled her to him. "I thought they'd killed you," she murmured into his shoulder.

"They were about to try."

Angus gently moved her back just a little. Their eyes locked. Relief and understanding sparked between them. Then he lowered his head and their lips met in a kiss.

After what seemed like a lifetime and also the blink of an eye, a polite cough sounded beside them.

"Sorry to interrupt your beautiful reunion," said Simon, "but we need to take everyone back to shore."

They reluctantly let go of each other and the boat rolled on a wave. Charlotte clutched her stomach and made a face. "I think I'm going to—"

She grabbed the railing and vomited over the side of the yacht.

"Come on, I'll take you below deck," Angus urged, leading Charlotte down the steps. "The sway isn't as bad down there."

Charlotte did as he asked and found herself in a cabin. Angus switched the lights on and got her to lie on the bed. "There's a toilet and sink in there. If you need to throw up again, it would be better for forensics if you could do it in those."

Charlotte put herself into the foetal position and groaned. "I need to get off this hellhole."

Angus sat next to her and stroked her hair. "I can't believe you're on a boat."

"Had to find you," she managed to say, her eyes shut.

It seemed to take an extraordinarily long time to get back to Exmouth Quay. The coastguard piloted the yacht, as the crew were kept below deck.It was only when she got back on dry land that the implications of Angus being on the yacht hit her.

"What happened?" she asked, as the coastguard team and the police milled about. "Someone must have hit you hard. You have a cut on your cheek, and it's swelling up."

Angus touched his cheek and winced."I thought the coastguard might be more of the gang turning up. Those gorillas on board tried to make Lawrence kill me."

"What? Bastards!" Charlotte looked about, a murderous glare on her face. Then she looked woebegone. "Oh God, if we'd been a little later, you might be floating facedown in the sea by now."

Angus took hold of her hand. "But I'm not."

Charlotte looked down at her feet. "I'm on dry land, but I still feel like I'm on the boat." She took a step and almost fell over. "When does the swaying stop?"

"How did you make it out to the Channel without getting seasick?" Angus asked, smiling at her.

"I don't know. I do get seasick, but I was on a mission. Maybe mind over matter helped. I couldn't think about being seasick when I didn't know what had happened to you. That was all I could focus on."

Simon walked over to them. "The thugs and Cameron have been taken to the station. I'll need statements from you both, of course." He turned to Charlotte. "Are you feeling any better now?"

She shook her head. "I need to go and lie down in a dark room."

"You did very well. I didn't think you got seasick at all until you, um... I'll get a police car to drop you home."

"My car's over there, but I don't think I can drive. Maybe in an hour—"

"I'll drive you home, Charlotte," Angus said. "And if it's all right with you, I'll head home in it myself."

Charlotte took his hand and smiled.

"I'll be in touch about statements," Simon said, beating a retreat.

Angus dropped Charlotte home and called Helena to look come and look after her.

When Helena arrived, she had concern all over her face.

"Vat happen?" She burst into Charlotte's bedroom where Charlotte had resumed the foetal position.

Angus explained briefly.

"You on boat!" Helena stood, her hands on her hips.

"Vat you do on boat?" She tutted, then huffed, then went into the en-suite and started the shower.

"Zank you, Mr Angus. I deal with her now. She need cold shower to snap her out of it. It work every time." Helena gave him a stern look not to argue, and waited for him to leave.

Chapter Thirty-Six

At 3.55pm the next day, Charlotte walked towards Lawrence's restaurant on the seafront in Exmouth.

Earlier in the day, she'd had a text from Angus: *Meet me at Oceanique at 4pm?*

The ping as the text arrived had rudely awakened her from a deep slumber. The adrenaline from the night before, and the fact Angus had kissed her, had kept her awake for hours. Had he kissed her, or had she kissed him? It was all a blur. But whoever had instigated it, he hadn't pulled away. That gave her hope.

Now, as she approached the restaurant, she wondered why Angus hadn't come to pick her up in her Volvo, and why, apart from the text about Oceanique, there had been radio silence from him since he'd dropped her home the night before.

She peered inside the restaurant. Angus, Cressida and Lawrence were sitting at one of the tables. She wondered how long they'd been sitting there talking without her, and a sudden wave of annoyance swept over her at being left out.

She knocked on the window and Cressida got up and unlocked the door. "Come in," she said.

Charlotte sat at the table and Angus smiled at her.

"Hello, Angus. Have you had that looked at yet?" She indicated his bruised cheek.

Angus shook his head. "It looks worse than it feels. You haven't officially met Lawrence, have you?"

"No."

Lawrence looked tired, though his wild hair from the night before was now tamed and he'd had a shave. He smiled faintly at Charlotte but didn't say anything.

"How long have you been here?" Charlotte asked Angus, unable to keep the note of accusation out of her voice.

"Just a few minutes."

"Well!" said Cressida, putting her palms on the table. "What an interesting night you all had yesterday. I'm almost jealous that I missed out on all the action."

Charlotte shot Cressida a look, but she didn't notice.

"Alls well that ends well," Angus said.

"You got yourself into a right old mess," Charlotte said to Lawrence. "An affair, debts *and* people-smuggling. Cooking up a fish supper will be boring for you, compared to the last few weeks."

Lawrence looked sheepish, then sighed. "I know I messed up big style."

"Would you care to explain exactly how and why you got involved in people-smuggling?" Charlotte narrowed her eyes at him.

Lawrence coughed. "I made a few bad investments. I didn't tell Cressy about them. A friend had a vineyard and I was going to have my own label, but the bad weather we had last summer meant the yield was ruined."

"You invested in an English vineyard?" Charlotte shook her head in exasperation.

"He was a friend, and it wasn't his fault the weather was bad."

"You won't find bad weather like that in the South of France or Italy. Plenty of vineyards to invest in there."

Lawrence ran his fingers through his hair. "It wasn't just that. I was persuaded to put money into a promising tech startup. They said they were going to revolutionise how restaurants handle inventory and waste. But they folded. Something about the techie's costing too much."

Charlotte sighed. Angus put his hand on hers and gave her a meaningful look that said *Don't say anything*. She took the hint and stayed silent.

Lawrence glanced at his wife and she smiled back. "Cressy has forgiven me. That's all that matters."

"So we should forgive you too?" Charlotte shot back. "I don't usually want to kill clients, but you almost got Angus killed!"

Lawrence cleared his throat. "Well, um, he wasn't, and we both put up a fight against those thugs."

"That's true," Angus said. "Lawrence helped subdue the thug who did this." He pointed to his cheek.

Charlotte narrowed her eyes, her murderous feelings deflated just a little.

Angus took an envelope from his jacket pocket and pushed it across to Cressida. "This is my invoice."

She took it without opening it. "I'll pay it straight away. Then Laurie and I will go away for a few weeks and try to make a fresh start. I know I've been working him too hard." She turned to him and put her hand on his. "I do love you very much, you know. You're more important than all this."

Lawrence looked down, then nodded.

"You're both welcome at the restaurant any time," Cressida added. "I really am so grateful to you. He would have ended up at the bottom of the English Channel if it wasn't for you both. Despite all this silliness, I love him to pieces."

"You can thank Kaylee, a teenage runaway," Charlotte said. "She warned me about the people-smugglers and she saw Angus being taken onto the boat. She's agreed to see me later, and I'll try and persuade her to accept my help."

"Tell her she can have a job here any time she likes."

"I will."

A few minutes later, on the seafront, Charlotte stopped dead. "We need to talk about what happened on the boat."

"The fight and rescue, or the fact that you kissed me?"

Charlotte's eyebrows shot up. "*You* kissed *me*."

Angus shook his head. "You definitely instigated it."

"You didn't seem to mind. And you didn't reject me like you did the first time." Charlotte bit her lip and glanced away. Angus considered. "But you threw up almost immediately afterwards."

Charlotte blushed. "That was the boat's fault."

Angus raised his eyebrows, still smiling, and Charlotte folded her arms. "All right, then. Kiss me again. That'll prove I threw up because of the boat."

Their eyes locked. Angus moved closer, put his hand on her cheek, and lowered his head. Their arms moved around each other and time stood still again.

Someone whistled and shouted, "Get a room!"

They broke apart and looked up as a small group of teenagers walked towards them, laughing.

"See, not even a retch..." Charlotte murmured in Angus's ear.

Once the teenagers had passed, Angus led her to a bench and they sat down.

"Is this when you tell me it won't work and we'd be better off as friends?" Charlotte asked.

"What? No!" Angus scanned her face. "What do *you* want?"

"I'd have thought that was obvious. I don't kiss my friends."

Angus's face was confused. "You do. What about Ross?"

Charlotte sighed. "All right, well, yes, Ross is a friend and sometimes more. But that's never been serious. He knows that. And anyway, the first time me and you kissed, you rejected me."

"You were drunk. I'd never take advantage of a woman incapable of giving consent."

"Always the gentleman." Charlotte considered. "Does that mean that if I'd kissed you that night sober, you wouldn't have turned me down?"

Angus smiled. "We'll never know. But it didn't take me long to feel more than friendship for you."

Charlotte's eyes widened. "Really? How long?"

"Oh, I'd have to give that some thought," he said, his smile broadening. Then the smile faded. "Look, we have a great work partnership. If it went pear-shaped and ended, I don't know what I'd do. If this is going to be more than work, more than a friendship, we need to make it work."

"I feel the same. And just for the record, I fancied you the moment I saw you on my doorstep with that laptop."

Angus grinned. "Really?"

"Yep. And it's been torture trying to keep my hands off you. I could have given up on my calls to Misty a long time ago if we'd got together sooner."

"Really?"

"Ask Helena." Charlotte gasped. "Oh my goodness, I

haven't told her yet. She'll be incandescent with happiness. Then annoyed that I didn't tell her straight away. I need to tell her." She took out her phone.

He put his hand on her phone. "Do it later. A bit longer won't hurt."

Charlotte consented and put her phone back in her bag.

"I suppose I better got to the police station and give my statement. Have you done yours?"

"Yes, I went earlier. It was a hive of activity. They had Cameron, Olivia, their goons and a number of others."

Angus's phone rang. He looked at the display. "It's my mum."

Charlotte sighed. "You can't not answer the phone when it's your mum. Go on."

He accepted the call. "Hi, Mum, how are you both?"

Charlotte got up and walked a few feet away to give him some privacy.

"Yes, I'm okay. You want me to come tonight? With Charlotte?" He glanced at Charlotte. She shrugged, and nodded. "Sure, I'll bring Charlotte. The Morris dancing finals? Oh yes, I'm sure she'll love it." And he grinned at Charlotte's reaction. She looked like she'd bitten into a lemon.

He ended the call. "First, though, I have a property to look at. It's a flat near the town centre here. It needs a lot of work, but it's owned by a friend of a friend who wants it off his hands asap. So no auction, no bidding war, no being outbid. Want to come along?"

Charlotte smiled. "I'd love to."

THE END

. . .

Acknowledgements:

Many thanks to my amazing husband for his constant support and encouragement. Also to Liz Hedgecock my editor and Paula, my proofreader.

About the Author

I started writing around 2002 starting with fan fictions. I then branched out into writing my own characters and stories, and in 2019 wrote the first Lockwood and Darrow book after Charlotte and Angus wouldn't get out of my brain unless I wrote them down. Although, as you can see, they are still there a lot of the time!

Like Charlotte, I grew up in Hertfordshire, and moved to Devon twenty years ago. It has had a profound affect on me because every book I've ever written has been set, or partly set in Devon.

I live close to the sea with my husband, three sons and two cats.

When I'm not writing, I love swimming and playing the violin.